The Pirate Queen

By

Joy Eileen

COPYRIGHT

Published by Joy Barnett

Published: Joy Eileen 2026

Formatting by: Joy Eileen

Proof read,, Edited by: Lawrence Editing Group

Cover SG Designs

Dedication

To the girls who were reading dirty books when they were way too young. This one is for you!

2nd Dedication

To the girls at that fateful table

KC Moon

MJ

Heather

&

Teri

Table of Contents

Prologue

Jack Bellamy is the most handsome man, Charlotte Fitzwilliam thought as she observed him manipulate a piece of rope into a complicated knot. Charlotte blushed at the thought. A thought she'd been having more frequently with each passing day.

Jack was more than his handsome features. He was Charlotte's saving grace, and she knew she needed to stop her wayward thoughts before she ruined the only friendship she held dear. The only friendship she'd ever really had.

Jack had come into Charlotte's life a year ago when she was in the depths of despair. Her mother had died giving birth to her younger brother, leaving Charlotte with no one to turn to with her tender, broken heart. Her father sank into himself, grieving his wife and unborn son. Her older brother, Alexander, never paid any attention to her. Even the staff seemed to have forgotten the young girl in their own grief.

Alexander was ten years her senior and never showed the brotherly instincts she'd read about in books.

She was utterly alone.

When the aching loneliness had been too much for Charlotte to handle, she'd secreted away to the loft in her father's stable. The stable loft had become her haven. The soft whinny of the horses and the smell of hay were comforting to her bruised heart. While she was in her sanctuary, Jack, the newest stable hand, had found her one fateful morning. The morning when Charlotte was no longer alone.

Charlotte had woken up morose one gloomy morning and sneaked out to her secret place. Although it wasn't truly sneaking out when nobody thought of looking for that person to ensure they were where they were supposed to be. The gray sky matched her mood, and not even her favorite book could bring her solace. She missed her mother. She missed the man her father used to be. She didn't really miss Alexander.

A shuddering sob broke out of Charlotte. Her young soul cracked from the brutality of her life. This was the first time Charlotte cried for her mother and the stability she had lost.

She hadn't been allowed to cry after she'd lost her mother and little brother. Her father's sister, Aunt Mira, pinched Charlotte on the back of the arm every time she looked as if she was about to show emotion. Aunt Mira frequently lectured her on the proper decorum of a lady. Always adding snide comments that Charlotte's parents raised an uncultured heathen when it came to her. Yet, Alexander was the epitome of proper behavior all marquesses should possess.

Aunt Mira's appearance was nothing like her brother's, Charlotte's father. Aunt Mira was a tall, waiflike woman with a pinched expression on her face when Charlotte was around. Charlotte wanted to know if she sucked on Cook's coveted lemons. Charlotte's father used to be a robust man who'd pick her up and spin her around until they were both gasping for air from laughing.

Now her father was never without his odious drink. His stomach increased while his hair decreased. He appeared gaunt and lost. All she wanted to do was hold him, tell him she was still there. But it appeared the whole family was going to mourn alone or at least without her.

Aunt Mira had taken full advantage, grumbling Charlotte's inadequacies when Charlotte's father wasn't within hearing distance. Charlotte wondered if her father would have championed her if Aunt Mira had listed her failures in front of him, or would he continue to drink his liquor, ignoring the world around him as he was now apt to do?

Alexander's smug expression every time Aunt Mira set her down made it obvious that he was, in fact, in hearing distance. By the grace of all that was holy, Aunt Mira was finally departing. Her bags were loaded, and she would soon be gone. Charlotte had foolishly hoped that with Aunt Mira making her departure, she'd feel better. That not being harped on with every move and disparaged with even the slightest show of emotion would somehow bring some semblance of right back into her very wrong world.

Charlotte thought wrong.

As the coach clomped away from the estate, Charlotte lost all hope that Aunt Mira was the root of all her problems. Charlotte's loneliness enveloped her. She felt as if she were drowning in heartache and nobody was there to save her.

Even the staff had drawn into themselves, ignoring young Charlotte, leaving her to navigate life without their normal liveliness. Cook no longer sang in the kitchen, and Jasper, their long-time butler, walked around as if all life had been drained from him after the mistress of the estate was laid to rest.

Charlotte curled into herself. Her knees pressed against her chest as she lay on the blanket she'd pilfered from the house when one of the maids wasn't looking and sobbed. She stifled her cries, not wanting Mr. Dons, the creepy stable master, to hear her. He was one staff member who Charlotte wouldn't mind if she never received a modicum of attention from again. He made her uncomfortable the way he watched her, licking his blackened teeth while he rubbed his rotund belly when she tended her horse, Cassiopeia. She wanted to tell her mother about Mr. Dons, but her mother fell ill, and Charlotte didn't want to disturb her. She'd always assumed she would tell her mom after the babe was born. And now she was gone.

A creak of the ladder made Charlotte's head shoot up. Had she conjured Mr. Dons by thinking of the lecherous fiend?

A thatch of curly black hair popped through the opening first. Definitely not Mr. Dons's greasy gray hair. Charlotte stared with watery eyes as the most beautiful boy she'd ever seen shimmied his way through the small opening.

His light brown eyes reminded Charlotte of her father's favorite drink. Charlotte had once sniffed the tumbler of the mesmerizing liquid. The smell burned her nose and had her coughing quietly as she ran out of her father's study before he caught her. The smell did not match the liquid's beauty. Charlotte wondered if this boy's beauty was also not going to match, the same way her father's scotch did. Both the boy and the drink were beautiful to look at, but would he burn her if she got too close?

The way life had been battering her lately, she wouldn't have been shocked if he was sent here to torment her by some divine being to make sure she wouldn't have an ounce of hope left in her life.

"Are you okay?" he asked in a whisper as he sat on the bare wood floor. He appeared as if he wanted to comfort her but was too afraid to get closer.

"Who are you?" Charlotte wanted to sound confident, like the daughter of a duke, but her question came out raspy and small.

"I'm Jack, the new stable hand. I was hired right before the lady of the house—" Jack stopped speaking when Charlotte sucked in an uneven breath, her eyes filling with tears she couldn't wish away.

"She was my mother. She is my mother. I mean..." Charlotte's throat clogged with tears, unable to finish her sentence.

Without a word, Jack scooted over cautiously, his gaze never leaving Charlotte's until he was right next to her. With guarded movements, he wrapped his strong arms around her, and to her utter embarrassment, Charlotte collapsed against his chest and let out a heart-wrenching sob that once started, it refused to be quelled.

"It's okay. Let it out." Jack's hand rubbed up and down Charlotte's back as she allowed her grief to pour out of her.

Sapped of all energy and tears, Charlotte leaned on Jack's wet shirt, unable to move from the emotional upheaval she'd expelled.

"I'm sorry," she hiccupped through her apology, but she wasn't sure what else to say.

"There's nothing to be sorry about. Do you want to talk about it?"

Charlotte remained quiet after his question, wondering if she wanted to unburden the past month to a complete stranger. A complete stranger who had been nicer to her than her wretched family. With a watery breath, Charlotte once again expelled her feelings, but this time in words. She explained how her father had shrunk into himself, how her vile aunt degraded her at every turn, how Alexander reveled in every hateful word her aunt spewed, and mostly how alone she felt.

Jack didn't say a word as she spoke, allowing everything to pour out of her body. He tensed when she explained the vitriol her aunt had spewed at her while her brother smugly watched. Yet, his hand never ceased its soothing path over her spine. When she was done, Charlotte felt lighter than she had since her mother took to her bed.

"You're not alone anymore. I'm here now."

Charlotte closed her eyes and allowed his words to settle over her battered heart.

"I have nobody either," he explained. "My mom died giving birth to me, and my father was killed over a year ago. We can be each other's family."

Charlotte snuggled further into his chest, feeling at peace.

"I'm sorry you have no family, but as awful as it sounds, I'm grateful that you're here with me," she whispered her confession into his chest, her body going limp from the emotional turmoil she'd endured.

"I'm glad too. I know what it's like to be alone, but I do have to go. Mr. Dons will fire me if I don't finish my duties before he gets to the stables."

Charlotte wanted to argue. She had just found her peace and the thought of letting him go seemed reprehensible. She wanted to tell him that she would beg her father to remove the horrid stable master from the estate in order for her to have more time with Jack. But even as the thought wandered through her mind, she knew it would be useless.

"Meet me here tonight after your family retires."

Charlotte nodded against his chest. At her agreement, he removed his hand from her back and gently put her on her makeshift bed.

"Are you going to be all right until tonight?" Jack's gaze wandered over Charlotte's face as if categorizing every nuance.

Charlotte opened her mouth but snapped it closed. She allowed herself to truly think about Jack's question, not wanting to give him false platitudes.

"Yes, yes, I will be all right." The odd thing about it was Charlotte did feel as if she'd be fine.

"You're a strong girl. What's your name?"

"Charlotte."

The side of Jack's mouth hitched up and Charlotte returned it with a small smile of her own.

"See you tonight." With that, Jack disappeared through the small opening.

Charlotte listened to him as he descended the ladder, the small smile refusing to leave her face. She wasn't alone any longer and Charlotte felt as if the world wasn't falling apart after all.

The day went by with the slowness that had Charlotte almost tearing her hair out. The clock ticked with a beat that was excruciatingly loud to her ears. She'd never wished for a day to be over with more than she had that day.

After her father had quarantined himself in his study with his bottle, Alexander slunk off to his club as soon as dinner was cleared away. The day was finally over.

Charlotte dismissed her lady's maid as soon as her hair was plaited. Immediately after she took her leave, she thrust her arms through her wrapper and left her room. With stealth, her slippered feet whispered past her father's study. Charlotte's rapidly beating heart sank when she realized he wouldn't have a single thought about her as soon as the amber liquid hit his tongue, or most likely before.

Charlotte ran as quickly as her young legs would take her. The damp grass soaked into her slippers, but even with frozen toes, she wouldn't slow. She surveyed the stables to ensure Mr. Dons wasn't sulking around in the darkness like some fairy-tale monster. When she ensured the creepy stable master wouldn't catch her, she lunged to the ladder and hoisted herself up.

Jack was already waiting for her when she reached the top.

"Fancy seeing you here, Lottie," he said with his crooked smile.

Charlotte's smile almost hurt her face. The loneliness surrounding her heart lifted at the sight of his dazzling face.

“I didn’t think today was ever going to end,” she admitted.

“It did seem to slow after I left you. Here.” He handed her a thick blanket that she immediately wrapped around her chilled shoulders.

“What would you like to do tonight?” he asked when she was situated.

“I don’t know. I just don’t want to be alone anymore. Alexander was particularly mean tonight and explained the reason my father refuses to look at me is because I resemble my mother too much and it hurts him. I’m tired of being lonely.”

Jack’s unusual brown eyes softened at her confession. His black hair had been combed back as if he tried to tame the unruly curls. They were not so easily tamed and already were revolting around his ears.

“We’ll never be alone again. We have each other now. Friends for life.” Jack reclined against the wall, his legs stretched out in front of him, crossing them at the ankle.

“Friends for life,” Charlotte repeated as her eyes stung with tears.

“Hey, no more crying.”

Charlotte nodded as she wiped her tears away with the back of her hand. "I don't mean to cry. I just miss my mom. I miss my family, and I didn't think I'd have a friend ever again."

"Well, you do. I didn't realize how much I needed a friend as well until I found you up here. It was as if you were sent here to make me feel less lonely."

Charlotte leaned against the wall opposite Jack, the blanket warming her as much as Jack's words.

"Now that we've decided that we're friends and will no longer be lonely. What would you like to do?"

"Sleep," she answered honestly as she snuggled further into the blanket. "Ever since my mother died, I haven't been able to sleep. I wake up from nightmares that I can't remember, but I know they are horrible."

"A bedtime story it is. Get comfortable and I'll tell you a story." Jack folded the blanket Charlotte had stashed up there and moved toward her. Charlotte lifted her head as Jack placed the blanket under it. "Comfortable?"

Charlotte nodded, her eyelids already growing heavy. Being in Jack's presence gave her a sense of safety and she was finally able to relax.

"Do you know anything about Greek mythology?"

"If you want to leave," Charlotte began.

"Stop, no more nonsense, Lottie. I don't mind letting some small-minded scourge feel as though he is stronger than me. He doesn't bother me, and as long as he's paying attention to me, he'll leave you alone. I do not trust him around you."

"I know, Jack. I don't trust him either."

They stared at each other, having a silent conversation where promises were made and an understanding was established.

The summer days melted together. Charlotte and Jack moved out of the stifling heat of the stable loft to the outdoors. They climbed trees, went swimming, and walked around the garden, sometimes sneaking out when the sun was still up.

Charlotte evaded her lady's maid, hoping that Jack would be able to get away from Mr. Dons so they could have a daylight adventure. Charlotte stealthily moved around the house, skirting the places she knew Mr. Dons might be.

Charlotte smiled when Jack's deep laughter reached her ears. She hurried faster in the direction of his voice, only to skid to a stop when she saw the new scullery maid, Mary, lean up and kiss Jack on the mouth. Charlotte waited for Jack to push her away, and when he didn't, Charlotte barely kept from casting up her accounts.

Charlotte ran, not worrying about being stealthy, but also not paying attention to where she was fleeing.

"Where are you running to, Lady Charlotte?" Mr. Dons sneered when she almost collided with him.

"I was on my way to the kitchen. Cook has a new pastry she wanted me to try." The lie felt stilted to her ears, but she needed to get away.

"I won't keep you, but I wanted to show you something with Cassiopeia." The disgusting man smirked, flashing his rotted teeth.

Charlotte's heart stuttered, which surprised her because after seeing Jack with the harlot maid, she didn't think her heart would be intact enough to feel anymore.

"What's the matter with Cassie?" she asked, worried about her beloved horse.

"Come, Lady Charlotte. She may need to be put down."

Without thinking, Charlotte followed him into the stable. All the warnings Jack had pushed into her head disappeared as she feared for her horse, and the confusion of seeing Jack kiss the nasty Mary made her less vigilant.

Charlotte was so worried about her horse that she didn't recognize the danger until it was too late. Cassiopeia was in her stall, chomping on hay as if all was right in the world.

Charlotte turned to run, but Mr. Dons was directly behind her.

"Where are you going? I wanted to talk to you." His leering smile put his blackened teeth on full display.

"I told you. Cook is waiting for me."

"I don't think that's true. Nobody in that whole bloody house gives any thought to you. Not one of them even knows where you are or cares where you are, for that matter."

The nausea churning in Charlotte's stomach from being stuck alone with Mr. Dons increased at the truth of his words. The only one who cared about her was kissing a floozy of a maid.

How long does kissing last? Will he be done soon?

His thick, meaty hands wrapped around her throat, squeezing as he moved her back into an empty stall. Charlotte struck out as Jack taught her. When her foot connected with the squishy parts between his legs, he cried out, throwing her against the wall. Charlotte sucked in ragged breaths, each one more painful than the one before.

"You'll regret that," he rasped out as he held his bullocks in his hands.

"No, you'll regret that."

Charlotte's head snapped up at the sound of Jack's menacing voice. It was the voice she had grown to love, but it had something in it that she'd never heard before. Something sinister and terrifying. She'd always felt safe with Jack, and she still did, but if she were Mr. Dons, she'd be scared beyond life.

"You stupid boy, this doesn't concern you."

A loud clang rang out, echoing against the stall walls. Mr. Dons's body went limp, bouncing against the hay-covered floor.

"Lottie, are you hurt?" Jack's hands roamed inches above her body as if he were afraid to touch her.

"I'm fine. You got here before he could do damage."

Charlotte's eyes flooded with tears and her body shook. Jack pulled her into his arms as Charlotte sobbed into his neck, just as she had when they first met.

"You're safe. I will always keep you safe, Lottie."

"Should we get out of here before he wakes?"

"Lottie, he's not going to wake."

Charlotte moved so she could look, but Jack kept her head anchored to him, not allowing her to see Mr. Dons's corpse.

"Is he dead?"

"Lottie, I need you to go inside, and I don't want you to come back out until tomorrow."

"No, Jack. They need to know what happened. They need to know why you did what you did. You shouldn't be punished for this. You were protecting me." Panic swelled in her swollen throat.

"It will all be fine, Lottie. I need you to go inside, and when they ask you what happened, tell them. Promise me you won't come out until tomorrow."

Jack moved her an arm's length away so they could make eye contact. His amber brown eyes and her bright blue ones connected.

"Promise me."

Charlotte nodded. Jack kissed her on the forehead before shuffling her out of the stall, not allowing her to look at the body cooling on the floor.

When Charlotte walked out of the stable, she knew in her broken heart that she would never see Jack again.

Chapter One

Ten years later

"My lady, His Grace is requesting you in the study." Mary, Charlotte's annoying harlot of a lady's maid, interrupted her musings.

The day Alexander had promoted Mary to Charlotte's personal maid, she'd begged to have her removed. The girl was cruel to Charlotte after—Charlotte stopped her mind from wandering in that particular direction—but it still didn't quell the need for Mary to resign her post. She hated the girl and was going to dismiss her as soon as she found Alexander on a good day where he would grant her request.

Charlotte took a deep breath and smoothed her clammy palms down her scratchy black dress. It surprised her that her brother remembered she resided in the house. In fact, she didn't think she'd ever see him again after their father's death.

Yet, there he was.

Alexander sat behind their father's desk as if he belonged there. Charlotte realized he did belong there, and it was his desk now. Her heart sank seeing him perched behind the desk with his impeccable posture confirming she would never reconcile with her father. He was lost to her when her mother died and never came back, exactly like Jack.

"Charlotte, please greet our guest, Lord Sterling," Alexander bit out like he was already annoyed with her presence.

Charlotte startled. She'd been focused on her brother taking his place in their father's spot and hadn't noticed their neighbor Lord Sterling sitting in the seat in front of the desk. Lord Sterling was an aging octogenarian who had been old when Charlotte was a child. His estate butted up against theirs, yet he was rarely seen due to his bouts of gout. He had outlived his two wives, both of whom were unable to produce an heir. There was much speculation that their lives had not ended naturally.

"Lord Sterling, please excuse my rudeness. I hadn't seen you there."

Lord Sterling's arthritic hands clenched on the arm of the chair as he rose to greet her. "Lady Charlotte, you are looking as lovely as ever."

"Thank you, my lord." She performed a graceful curtsy, all the while wondering why Alexander had summoned her.

"Charlotte, I wanted to inform you that Lord Sterling and I have just signed the marriage contract."

Charlotte cocked her head with confusion. Her thoughts stuttered and her body felt heavy with dread, but there was no possible way her brother would do something so despicable. "Congratulations, my lord. May I ask who the lucky lady is?" It took everything in Charlotte not to say the poor, unfortunate soul instead of lady.

Lord Sterling chuckled, causing him to go into a coughing fit. When Lord Sterling recovered, he wheezed, "Why, my dear, it is you who is the lucky lady."

Charlotte whipped her head around and stared at Alexander, her mouth hanging open in disbelief. Alexander's blue eyes were hard and filled with hatred, silently telling Charlotte she had no options.

Charlotte gulped down the bile crawling up her throat as Lord Sterling grinned at her with his missing teeth.

"I apologize, my lord, I was unaware of this arrangement and it has caught me by surprise."

"Don't worry, Lady Charlotte, His Grace has explained that he wanted to wait until the marriage negotiations were complete and the marriage contract had been signed before informing you. I can see how this may have come as a shock," Lord Sterling confessed.

"Yes, I assure you, His Grace was surely thinking of my delicate sensibilities in this matter, as I am still in mourning." Charlotte nodded toward her black dress as if she needed it to prove her point. "Which, as you know, I will be observing for a year."

"I'll not be having my bride wearing black at our wedding next week." Lord Sterling spoke to Alexander, no longer giving Charlotte his attention.

"Of course, Lord Sterling. I will send out to have Charlotte outfitted in a dress befitting your joining," Alexander soothed Lord Sterling as Charlotte's ears started to ring at the mention of her upcoming wedding, which was apparently happening in one week.

One. Week.

Lord Sterling and Alexander spoke for a moment longer as Charlotte focused diligently on not allowing the black spots dotting her eyes to grow and pull her under.

Lord Sterling kissed the back of her hand as the butler was rung and showed him out. When the door closed, Charlotte stood, needing to make herself taller so she would be seen and not ignored.

"Do not start with theatrics, Charlotte. Really, will you ever comport yourself as a lady should?"

"What is the meaning of this? I'm not marrying him, Alexander. His last two wives died of suspicious circumstances after not producing him an heir. I refuse to be the third."

"Yes, you are, Charlotte. If I have to carry you down the aisle kicking and screaming, which I wouldn't put it past you and your heathen ways, I will."

Charlotte sank into the chair Lord Sterling had just vacated, her legs no longer able to hold her up. "Why? Why are you doing this to me? He's a horrible man who has most likely killed twice already, if not more. Do you hate me that much?"

"Why?" Alexander roared. "Because you are finally able to make yourself useful. It seems Father died with considerable debt. Most of it to Lord Sterling. When Lord Sterling came to collect his due, I offered you instead of payment and he accepted. This is very generous of him, Charlotte. He is taking on an unruly wife without a dowry and wiping the estate's debt. You will do your best to present him with an heir. If you are unable to do that simple task, it is your fate, and Lord Sterling can do with you as he sees fit. In one week, you will no longer be my problem. I will not hear any more about this. The seamstress will be here tomorrow, and you will be fitted for a yellow dress, which is your future husband's favorite color."

Charlotte recoiled at the thought of wearing yellow as if that was the worst of her problems. Yet, she looked awful in yellow. With her dark brown hair and blue eyes, yellow made her look sallow.

"Alexander, could you use my dowry to pay off Lord Sterling? I would much rather have it go to use in paying off Father's debts than have to marry him."

Alexander's jaw clenched and the hatred flashed in his eyes once again. "You have no dowry, Charlotte. You truly are a fool. Get out of my sight. I am done speaking of this."

"No dowry?" Charlotte asked as she wondered how many more revelations she'd have to endure that day.

"Dammit, Charlotte, do you ever listen?" Alexander stood up and stalked over to her, then pulled her by her upper arm in a brutal grasp. "I said to get out of my face. And know this, if you do anything to ruin this wedding, that hag you love so much will not only lose her home, she'll lose her life as well." He pulled her to the study door and tossed her out of the room, then slammed the door in his wake.

Charlotte stared at the heavy wooden door. The pain in her arm was nothing compared to the pain in her heart. She wanted to push her way back into the study and scream at Alexander that she refused to marry Lord Sterling. She would run away to London or the country to become a healer like Agatha. She'd have to take Agatha with her. She didn't trust Alexander not to hurt the old healer after he discovered she'd fled.

Charlotte had been studying with the old woman since the day she found her on the edge of the property. She was aware that if she took that path, she would most likely never get married and she would only be married to healing as Agatha was, but anything would be better than marrying Lord Sterling.

"Lady Charlotte, if you'd come with me. His Grace has asked me to take you to your room." Mary stood there with an odd look on her face.

Charlotte wanted to scream at her. She'd never grown to like Mary in the years she'd been her lady's maid, mostly because Mary was the one she saw kissing Jack all those years ago. Mary didn't hide her dislike for Charlotte either. She never came out and said it, but she blamed Charlotte for making Jack leave.

When Charlotte had explained to her father what had happened, Mary went into hysterics, and her father had her forcibly removed from the room. Her father called the constable, and Charlotte had to explain the whole ordeal again.

Her father never doubted her, but he didn't comfort her either. He simply put out an advert for a new stable master and continued to ignore Charlotte.

Alexander had then replaced her current lady's maid with Mary as soon as her father was too ill to make sound decisions. Mary would get her revenge on Charlotte by "accidentally" poking her with a hairpin, cinching her garments too tight, or forgetting to bring up her meal. Mary was just another way for her brother to make her life miserable.

"I think I'm going to take a walk around the garden, Mary. I will have my meal sent to my room, though." *It will be cold anyway*, Charlotte thought.

"I'm sorry, my lady, but as I said, His Grace has asked me to escort you to your room and as for your meal, he has also informed me that you will be taking the remainder of your meals in your room until the wedding." Mary could barely hide her glee.

Charlotte stared open-mouthed at her lady's maid as she digested her words. Mary had always been careful with her barbs, always on the precipice of being able to shrug it off as careless, but this was blatant aggression. Charlotte was going to argue, but a dawning awareness came to her. Mary had been oddly absent at certain times of the day, and when she wasn't, she had a silly smile plastered on her normally sour face. Charlotte was certain she knew where Mary had been sneaking off to and why she was so dedicated to Alexander's wishes.

Charlotte nodded as she headed toward the stairs, unsure what Mary would do if Charlotte dawdled any longer than she already had. Alexander had set all of this up and Charlotte was completely in the dark. He'd negotiated a wedding and most likely seduced her already horrid maid to do his bidding.

Charlotte was going to have to escape.

In the days up to her wedding, the only other person she saw besides Mary was the seamstress, who grumbled and stuck her with too many pins to be a coincidence. Mary never let her out of her sight, and when she was allowed a reprieve away from her traitorous maid, her door was locked.

Charlotte waited until the horrid maid took away her untouched food and Charlotte laughably dismissed Mary for the night, refusing her help in getting into her night clothes. She may have pretended to dismiss Mary, but they both knew Charlotte had no power.

When the house settled, Charlotte quietly lifted the window and shimmied down the side of the house. She'd perfected her escape route all those years ago in order to sneak out to see Jack. She hadn't had to use this route in many years, but thankfully, her muscle remembered the way to freedom.

She ran as quickly as she could to the edge of the property where old Agatha's tiny shack resided. Charlotte's breath pushed out of her when she saw the flickering of light through the tiny window. When she reached the shack, she knocked quickly, her stomach in knots. She just needed to see a friendly face.

Agatha's gnarled face appeared as the door swung open. "Come in, child."

Agatha moved and Charlotte noted the two steaming cups of tea on the small table. Charlotte's shoulders sank at the sight. Agatha had a way of knowing things before they happened. It was one of the reasons she was sought out for healing and other inquiries from all the neighboring estates.

Charlotte asked her once why she continued to live in the tiny shack when she had been offered a considerable amount of money for her medical and life advice. Agatha just patted her on the cheek as she explained she had no need for money and she was exactly where she was needed.

"Sit, drink." Agatha pointed her knobbed finger toward the tea.

Charlotte knew Agatha wouldn't talk until after she'd read her leaves. She obediently sat at the sturdy table and sipped her tea. The hot liquid did nothing to dispel the dread of her impending marriage.

No, she thought. She would not marry him. She would take Agatha and leave as soon as she finished her tea.

Charlotte set the cup down more firmly than she meant to. "Agatha, I need you."

"Hush." Agatha snatched her cup with agility her old body shouldn't have been capable of.

Charlotte bit her bottom lip, wanting to grab Agatha and make a run for it. She loved the old healer. She'd been her saving grace when Jack left.

After the constable left and she was dismissed from her father's library, Charlotte went in search of solace and she found it in the dilapidated shack. She'd never ventured toward the ramshackle shack before, yet something drew her to walk in its direction.

The sight of the small dwelling with comforting smoke drifting out of the rock chimney stopped her in her tracks. When she neared, Agatha opened the door, beckoning her in as if she'd been waiting for her, and maybe she had been.

That was the first day she had her tea leaves read and the beginning of their friendship. Every day after, Charlotte would make her way to Agatha's hut, where she learned the healing arts of herbs. Agatha made Charlotte her unofficial assistant, sending her on night chases to find a specific root or bark off a certain tree only to be harvested on a full moon.

Villagers, young, old, rich, and poor, found their ways to Agatha's door with numerous maladies and Charlotte was next to her, helping.

Charlotte tapped her foot on the clean floor as she waited impatiently for Agatha to finish reading her leaves. She opened her mouth to speak, but Agatha peered at her with her rheumy eyes before she could get a word out.

"You learned everything you'll need to know. You don't need old Agatha anymore."

"Agatha, listen to me. Alexander is selling me to Lord Sterling. We're to be married in two days. We need to leave immediately."

Agatha reached out and patted her hand. "Oh, child. You're about to go on a grand adventure. Remember you're strong. You've hidden your strength for too long. It's time for you to find the woman you are meant to be. It's not going to be easy, but trust in yourself."

Tears streamed down Charlotte's face as she gripped the old woman's hand. "Please, Agatha, we must leave. I'll sneak out tomorrow, and we will be out of here before Alexander knows I'm gone."

"You've had a lonely life, child. You'll no longer be alone. Trust in yourself and trust in your instinct."

"Fine, fine, I promise to trust my instinct. And at the moment, my instincts are telling me we need to get out of here tomorrow night. Please tell me you'll be ready."

Agatha squeezed her hand with more strength than she should have possessed. "All right, child. Get some rest. Our next adventure will start tomorrow."

At the old woman's words, the pressure on Charlotte's chest didn't abate as she thought it would. The whole trek back to the house, foreboding niggled at her, but she shook it off as worry.

The next night when she snuck out with her bags packed with everything of value, the heavy feeling of dread still hadn't dissipated. The hut stood as it always did, yet it felt as if all the life had been removed from it. She told herself the reason the ever-present smoke was gone was only because Agatha was getting ready for their escape.

When the door swung open at her knock, Charlotte already knew what she was going to find. A hole was slugged through her stomach when she took in the empty room. It was as if Agatha never existed. Charlotte walked into the room and gathered the mug she'd had drunk her tea from hundreds of times. It was the only thing that marked Agatha had, in fact, existed.

The dregs of her tea leaves formed a heart, which appeared to be mended with tiny stitches. Charlotte sank to the floor, clutching the mug, and allowed her anguish to take over. She sobbed, the mug digging into her chest as she held it closer, wanting to meld it into herself. Wanting the mended heart to take over whatever currently resided in her chest.

On shaky legs, Charlotte gathered her bags and trudged back to her prison of a room. She held the mug to her chest the rest of the night as sleep evaded her.

She wanted to be the strong woman Agatha thought she was, but Charlotte wasn't certain she could be anything else but a lonely girl with a broken heart.

Chapter Two

Charlotte's wedding day was upon her. Mary brutally shook her awake as the sun rose over the horizon. Charlotte shrugged her off without any care for the awful woman. If Charlotte was going to marry Lord Sterling, she wasn't going to be treated this way by a traitorous idiot who was going to be thrown aside by her brother at any moment.

Agatha's words rang in her ears as she pushed Mary off her when she moved to shake her again. She may not be the epitome of strength Agatha saw in her, but she wouldn't be the weak girl Mary thought she was.

Charlotte had resigned herself to this farce of a wedding. It would be easier to escape Lord Sterling than Alexander, and if Charlotte was lucky, maybe the old codger would die before he had a chance to end her life.

"You will not handle me like that again," Charlotte commanded the blonde shrew. Mary might blame Charlotte for making Jack leave, but what Mary didn't know was that

Charlotte blamed Mary just the same. "You may take your leave of me. I will ready myself for my wedding without your help."

"Lord Alexander told me not to take my eyes off you this day," Mary said with an air of superiority.

"You are a fool, Mary. I don't know what he promised you, but he will throw you out as soon as your usefulness is over. Do you really think he would lower himself to do anything with a servant except a small dalliance to get what he needed from you?"

Mary screamed and lunged toward Charlotte. Charlotte pulled back her hand and punched her square in the face just as Jack had taught her all those years ago. Blood spurted out of her nose and Mary's eyes went wide as she covered her face with her hands.

"Now you will leave me alone. I will be dressed and styled for the wedding, but I will not be seeing your face again."

Mary made her way out of her room, her nose dripping on the carpet. She hoped it stained the carpet enough that it had to be replaced.

Charlotte's heart sank faster than the rising sun. She silently begged for a way out of the situation she was in. She knew she was alone, and she wasn't naive enough to think someone was going to come to her rescue, but a plan to get out of her current predicament would've been nice.

Charlotte closed her eyes, picturing Lord Sterling waking up and having an apoplectic fit or pitching over as he made his descent down the stairs. Anything to keep him from arriving at the church.

With a deep sigh to rid herself of her murderous thoughts, she began getting ready for her wedding day.

She brushed her long dark hair until it shined after slowly walking around her rooms as if she were headed to the guillotine instead of her wedding.

Charlotte was thoroughly stumped. Her brown hair was up in a tight chignon, and she was ready, all except for the blasted yellow wedding dress. She had pulled it on and realized that she would be unable to button the ridiculously tiny buttons on the back of the dress without help. She stared at herself in the mirror. The hideous dress hung around her waist.

Her heart-shaped face and blue eyes under sharp dark eyebrows watched back in horror at what stood before her. With her hair in the sophisticated updo, she saw her mother staring back at her, and she understood why her father couldn't stand to be near her. Dressed, or half dressed as she was, she did resemble her mother to a terrifying degree. Her figure was similar as well. She was slight. Her hips and small breast developed later than the maids close to her age, but as she stood in front of the mirror, there was no denying she was a woman, and this was the last step to obliterating her childhood.

A horrible screech sounded from her sitting room. Charlotte held up to her bosom the hideous dress as she ran into the room to see what was causing the commotion.

Charlotte paused as a tarnished black boot pushed through the pulled-up window. Charlotte observed in horrified astonishment as a man clad in knee-high black boots, tan breeches, and a billowy white shirt, which was not fully buttoned, pushed his way through her window.

He gave her a gallant smile, but it was replaced by a look of disgust. "So, I see you're not only making poor choices in future husbands, but in dresses as well." His accent was different than any she'd ever heard. It had a touch of English to it but also a roughness that scraped against her ears.

"Who are you? And what are you doing in here?" Charlotte whispered, unsure if Alexander had servants listening at the door.

One hand was clamped on the back of a brocade settee, the only thing in between her and the intruder, as the other hand continued to hide what she could with the unbuttoned dress clutched to her.

The man glanced at the doorway as if he could read her mind about listening servants. Charlotte studied him quickly, her feet still frozen to the carpeted floor as she clutched the furniture. He was captivating with his bronze skin, which appeared as if the sun had worshipped him. His large, muscular shoulders dipped down to a hard physique, and from what his shirt revealed, his stomach resembled a washing board.

When Charlotte glanced up at him, she was startled to see he was studying her just as she did him. He wore a black scarf around his head, concealing not only his hair but shadowing his eyes as well. A scar ran down his face, ending in the middle of his cheek, but she was unsure where it began. His mustache and thick beard showcased his full lips. She wasn't sure why, but she thought he winked at her as he shot her with a grin. His white teeth were a stark contradiction to his tan face.

"Are you done with your assessment, Pet?" he asked, his smile widening.

"Once again, I ask who you are and what you are doing in my bedroom?"

"Why, I'm kidnapping you, of course."

"I beg your pardon?"

"Your pardon is denied."

Charlotte blinked at his words, unable to comprehend their meaning. Then the full understanding hit her, and her shoulders sank. This was not the rescue she'd wished for, and there was nothing more for it. "My brother will not pay a ransom. He would probably be grateful you're taking me off his hands. I suggest finding another person to steal your fortune from and allow me to get back to my wedding."

A rumbling chuckle reverberated in her ears, and the sound was not as displeasing as it should have been.

If Charlotte didn't know any better, she would have sworn sadness flitted across his features after his chuckle. He moved and Charlotte countered it by going the opposite way. His grin deepened and he took another step toward the other side of the settee. Once again, Charlotte moved away.

He huffed and shook his head, the jewelry around his neck glinting from the movement.

"Menace," he mumbled. Without another word, he went to her dressing room and began rifling through her closet. Charlotte finally moved but lost all sense when she followed him instead of running the other way. Why had she told him her brother didn't care for her? Would he sell her off as she'd heard tales of missing women? Would she have a better chance at escaping this man or Lord Sterling? She stopped her movement toward him and instead changed course toward her door.

"Don't even think about it," he said, coming out of her room with a sack over his shoulder and a simple morning dress clutched in his hand. "Put this on. I don't have much time." His voice brimmed with annoyance as if she were the one inconveniencing him. Anger rose in Charlotte's chest. She was not the annoyance in this situation.

He threw the dress at her, and Charlotte let it hit her in the chest and fall to the ground. After a quick assessment, she decided she would have better luck with the feeble Lord Sterling than the hulking man currently stalking toward her. Who knew, maybe he was done killing his infertile wives or he'd die before he could end her life.

"If you come any closer, I'll scream. It's my wedding day, and my betrothed would not take lightly to a man coming into my room and you will be shot, if not worse."

"I assume this is not the first time you've had a man in your room, and you can scream as loud as you want. I don't think your future geriatric husband would be able to hear you if he were standing right next to you."

Charlotte opened her mouth to scream, wondering if her brother would delay the wedding after he stopped this botched kidnapping. She wasn't even able to inhale before he was on her. Within a second, his rough, calloused hand pressed against her mouth. She bit down on the little flesh she could get in between her teeth, and he cursed as he roughly unhanded her. Charlotte moved to run to the door, but he caught her around the waist.

"Stop fighting me, Pet. I assume you can't be more ruined than you already are, but let's not tempt fate, shall we?"

In her attempt to escape, Charlotte's unbuttoned wedding dress sagged at her waist. His odd choice of words had her mouth hanging open in confusion, and the mad dash to her door had her panting. It was not from his hard body pressing against her. He stuffed a stocking in her gaping mouth with his free hand and pushed the hideous wedding dress down the rest of the way. The sound of ripping came from behind her before her hands were tied behind her back with what she could only assume was her ruined wedding dress.

"You had to do it the hard way," he muttered, pulling her to her bedroom.

Charlotte struggled as her bed loomed near. She couldn't pull in a full, deep breath with her mouth stuffed full of silk, and black dots danced before her vision. She ordered herself not to swoon. As he yanked the blanket from her bed in one swift tug, Charlotte struggled, not wanting him to wrap her in it. Her struggle was futile as he had the blanket snuggly wrapped around her before she could form a plan, which left her even more faint.

He hefted her up, and the air knocked out of her when his shoulder crammed into her stomach. With each step he took, she bounced, hindering her from taking in a full breath. His stride never faltered as if he didn't have a half-fainting woman in his arms. Charlotte attempted to escape, but the blanket thwarted all movement. A harsh crack landed on her backside.

"Stop struggling or I'll have no choice but to knock you out."

Charlotte remained silent and still, not because he commanded her to, but because she knew her door wouldn't be unattended, and this ruffian would be caught post haste. In her panic, she wasn't thinking clearly. There was no way this man would make it two steps out her door without being apprehended.

Except, he wasn't.

A loud commotion sounded downstairs, and it appeared to have everyone's attention.

"Impeccable timing. Now if you would be so kind as to hush as we make our escape, I would greatly appreciate it. That hideous dress gave me a megrim."

Charlotte couldn't believe the conceit of this man. Telling her to be quiet as he rushed her from the only home she had ever known, on her wedding day no less.

Screams and shocked voices filtered toward Charlotte as she bumped against the ruffian's shoulder with every step he took. She knew by the turns that he had taken her down the servants' stairs and not the main staircase. She wasn't hopeful that a servant would catch them with all the commotion going on.

His steps slowed and Charlotte wondered if she should try her escape now. With the house in an uproar, she might be able to get away from her kidnapper and Lord Sterling at the same time. Yes, she was fully aware she didn't have any references, but there had to be some way she could peddle her healing skills.

She didn't have any friends or acquaintances in London as she never got to attend a season. Her father fell ill when she was sixteen and she had nobody to sponsor her when the time arrived for her debut. Now she was in mourning, never having the opportunity to live without constraints.

She had been sequestered at the country estate and hadn't seen any of the world. Now it seemed that she was on an adventure where she assumed she'd travel farther than she'd ever ventured, and she couldn't see any of it as a blanket was obstructing her view.

Charlotte had the strange urge to go into hysterics. A bubble of laughter escaped past her silk stocking, but before another could leave her mouth, her kidnapper adjusted her on his shoulder, causing all the air to be expelled from her lungs.

"Oops, sorry about that, Pet."

Charlotte wanted to scream, but she knew it was useless. She was at the mercy of the man whose shoulder she currently resided on. Now she schemed in her blanket prison to pretend to be agreeable with him in the hopes he would realize she was worth no value and let her go.

"Cap'in, we need to get out of here," another voice Charlotte had never heard cautioned who she could only assume was her kidnapper.

"Here, take this, Jackal."

Charlotte listened as he handed off the bag he'd stuffed when he was rummaging through her clothes.

"Do you need help with the little bird?"

"No, nobody touches her," her kidnapper said with a deadly finality that had Charlotte's eyes widening.

What was he going to do to her?

Charlotte's blind world tilted as he lifted his leg and launched himself over what she could only assume was a horse. After shuffling her around, Charlotte was sitting with her legs draped over one side of the horse, still bundled in the blanket. Even with the layers between them, heat seeped into Charlotte from her kidnapper's muscular body as he wrapped an arm around her, anchoring her to his front.

They set off at a brutal pace, Charlotte bouncing hard against the saddle. With a huff, he pulled her even closer to him and pushed her head against his shoulder. She tried to fight, but it was useless. They rode for what Charlotte felt was hours. Her head hurt, her mouth was dry from the stocking, and she'd allowed fear to take over as she thought of different scenarios of her future, each one more dire than the last.

With the stuffiness of the blanket and the horrible thoughts going through her head, Charlotte struggled, panic infusing her.

"Stay still. We're almost there."

Charlotte stilled, wanting more than anything to get out of the stifling prison. After minutes went by, Charlotte thought he had lied to her and was about to continue struggling. She was no longer worried about being in his good graces, when he did, in fact, slow the horse.

"Jackal, go get us two rooms and food to be brought up. Come back here when you've obtained them."

"You've got it, Cap'in."

When the sound of Jackal's footsteps faded away, Charlotte was jostled off the horse. Cool air hit her face when he pulled the blanket from her body.

"Jackal is getting us a room. I'll untie you when we get to the room so you can eat and refresh, but only if you promise not to do anything stupid when we walk through the inn."

His shadowed eyes, still hidden with the black cloth, penetrated her as if drilling the order into her skull. Even though Charlotte couldn't see his eyes, she knew with certainty he was watching every minute movement she made.

Needing to get out of the blanket she was in and the stocking out of her mouth, she most likely would have agreed to anything he asked. She nodded.

"Ahh, so you can make good decisions. Behave, Pet."

He pulled the blanket away and Charlotte had a moment of relief, no longer being stuck in the prison, when she remembered she was only in her shift and petticoats. He chuckled as his eyes lingered on her body as no man had ever looked at her.

"Remember, not a word," he cautioned as he pulled the stocking from her mouth.

Charlotte swallowed convulsively, her parched mouth dry. She moved her jaw back and forth, wishing she could rub the soreness from her cheeks, but her hands were still tied behind her back.

"What are you going to do with me?" she rasped, her tongue sticking to the roof of her mouth at the end of the question.

"Let's get you dressed before Jackal gets back, shall we?" He purposely ignored her question as he led her over to the other horse and pulled the sack from it. After rifling around, he pulled out a dark blue dress. "This should do."

He untied her hands and tingling exploded throughout her arms. She sucked in a breath as pain overwhelmed her. Charlotte silently wished her arms would fall off so she wouldn't have to endure the blood rushing back into her limbs. She concentrated on lifting one foot and then the other to assist him in getting her dressed, but when he grabbed her arm to push it through the sleeve, she couldn't stop from crying out.

"What?" he asked, circling around as if there were an invisible threat.

"My arms." Was all she could stutter out before the sounds of Jackal's footsteps nearing reached them.

Charlotte allowed her captor to shove her tingling arms in the sleeves and hurry around to tie her stays. He grabbed her arms and shook them. The intensity of the pain almost brought her to her knees.

"Stop. Why are you doing this to me?" she whispered, tears trekking trickling down her cheeks.

"Give it a second and the tingling will stop."

She was about to unleash her sharp tongue when she realized he was correct and the pain was subsiding.

"All right, Cap'in, I got the rooms, and the food will be sent up shortly. I also got a bath sent up to your room for the bird," Jackal said with a toothless smile. "'Ello there, little bird."

Charlotte inclined her head. The man was huge, his gray hair pulled back in a long ponytail. He was just as tan as the captain, but his large body towered over the captain with his height. She couldn't understand why this gargantuan of a man was being so cavalier with the person he'd assisted in abducting.

Jackal's head cocked to the side as he studied her. "She's a pretty one for sure, Cap'in. And you said, we're to be taking her."

"That's enough, Jackal." The captain, as Jackal had called him, cut him off before he could reveal where they were taking her.

"Where are you taking me?" she asked. Her voice still hadn't recovered from the stocking.

"We're taking you to your room where you'll enjoy a bath. If it's hot or cold depends on how quickly you start moving. You'll eat, then go to bed because we leave early tomorrow to get to our destination," he answered as Jackal moved over to fetch the horses to lead the animals to the stables.

The captain grabbed one of her hands, lacing his fingers with hers. She startled at the contact and when she attempted to jerk free, he squeezed her fingers to stop her.

"Do not say a word, or I'll slit your throat before you can form a sentence," he hissed in her ear right before the stable boy came over and took the reins. "Give them both a good rubdown and extra oats," he told the boy, flicking a coin his way.

"They'll get the best treatment, sir," he said, stuffing the coin in his pocket before taking both horses.

"Good girl," he whispered in her ear.

Charlotte shivered from the praise as it caressed the back of her neck. She was disgusted at her reaction and shot him a dirty look. He grinned at her rage as they made their way to the inn.

Loud, boisterous voices hit her as soon as the door was open. Charlotte shrank back from the sound. Never being in society and living a quiet country life, the noise was too much to bear.

“Sorry, Pet, we couldn’t get you better accommodations on such short notice. Apparently, all the castles in the vicinity didn’t have any vacancies.” He all but had to yell for her to hear him over the din. He had interpreted her shying away from the noise as disgust at the inn.

She gritted her back teeth, knowing her throat was too abused to attempt to yell to be heard. Jackal walked in front with his head down, moving with more stealth than someone his size should.

Charlotte took the big man’s lead and put her head down as she went up the rickety wooden stairs with her hands still interlaced with the captain’s. Jackal opened one of the doors and ushered them in before ambling down two more rooms.

“See you in the morning, Cap’in and Little Bird.” Jackal’s eyes twinkled before he disappeared inside his room.

Once inside, Charlotte wrenched her hand free and almost toppled over when he didn’t fight the movement.

He moved to a table by the fireplace and plopped down in one of the two chairs before he began unlacing his boots.

"What are you doing?" Charlotte's eyes widened as his stockinged foot came into view.

"I'm getting comfortable." He didn't look up as he began on his other boot.

"You can't undress here. We shouldn't even be in the same room together. This is improper." She cringed at how much she sounded like her aunt Mira.

"Proper. You wish to lecture me on proper?" He threw off his shoe and stood before stalking over to her. His large frame was intimidating as he towered over her.

Charlotte couldn't help but thrust her chin up as she glared at him. "Yes, I will lecture you on propriety. Even a heathen like you should understand that it is improper to be alone together."

He pushed his hand up as if he wanted to run his fingers through his hair but stopped when he encountered the black material covering the top of his head.

"I think it's a little too late for propriety. Don't you?"

Charlotte couldn't be sure, but she would've sworn his gaze was pointed down toward her stomach.

“And whose fault is that? Stealing me away on my wedding day and forcing me to share a room with you was not what I requested today.”

He cocked his head as his attention intensified on her. “What did you request today?”

Heat coated the back of Charlotte’s neck, creeping around to the front. He waited as she refused to answer him.

“Did you request someone to save you from having to marry that wrinkled bollocks old codger?”

Charlotte had heard the word bollocks before, but it was always overheard, never spoken when they knew she was in the room. The fact that this man, this scoundrel, said it in front of her as if she weren’t raised to be a lady fueled her simmering anger. Charlotte knew she shouldn’t be surprised at his language—he’d kidnapped her—but for some reason, that word brought her reality to life.

Tears threatened the backs of Charlotte’s eyes. They burned as all the day’s events settled on her slight shoulders.

“Can you at least speak to me as if I’m a lady?” Her voice didn’t sound like her own. Her throat burned with the back of her eyes as she attempted to keep her tears at bay.

“Oh, excuse me, my lady.” He sketched a bow at her. “I forgot I was in the presence of royalty.”

"Why? Why are you doing this?" Charlotte begged.

"Answer my question first. What did you wish for today?"

Before Charlotte could answer, there was a knock on the door. Her apprehender thrust his hand over her mouth. "Not a word," he whispered. He stared at her until she nodded, and he slowly moved his hand off her mouth, one finger at a time.

The knock sounded again, this time more impatient than the first.

Charlotte watched warily as he pulled out a pistol from a pocket that she'd been unaware of until that moment. He hid the weapon behind his back as he gingerly opened the door as Charlotte held her breath.

"Your food and bath are here, sir." The annoyed voice of a young boy huffed as he entered the room with a large bucket of steaming water.

Another boy, almost identical to the first, went by and pulled the bathing tub that hung from the wall that sat in front of the fire. He'd then stirred the kindling to life with the flick of a match. The first boy dumped the steaming water in the tub while the second went out and grabbed another steaming bucket of water. This went on until the tub was over halfway full. As the last bucket was poured in, one of the twins, as Charlotte assumed they were, came in with a covered tray.

With their chores done, her abductor handed each a coin that had their dour faces splitting into large grins.

"Thank you, sir," they both said in unison. "Please, let us know if you need any further assistance."

"Get on with yourselves before my bath and food get cold," her captor grumbled and the two boys sprinted down the rickety stairs.

Her captor grinned but must have remembered she was in the room. His face went back to cold and calculating as he turned to her. "Would you like to bathe first?"

The idea of washing the grime from her body that had accumulated as she was rolled in that blanket sounded heavenly. "Yes." She stopped herself from saying "please" as she refused to offer any manners to this brutish man.

"All right, I'll go after."

Charlotte was embarrassed at the thought of sharing the same bath water, but with the option of going first, she wouldn't dwell on the intimacy of the act. She waited for him to leave the room so she'd have privacy to bathe. She frowned when he sat down and pulled the cover off the food the twins had set on the table.

"Well, what are you waiting for? The water is going to get cold, and it would be nice if I'd get some of the warmth."

"Aren't you going to leave?" she asked, tapping her foot against the wooden floor.

He barked out a laugh. "I'm not leaving you alone anytime soon. Now get in the bath. I would like to get some sleep before we leave in the morning."

"I'm not getting undressed with you in the room," she whispered, her knees going weak at the thought.

"You'll bathe even if I must do it for you. You smell like high heaven, and I'll not sleep next to you."

"Did you, did you just imply I stink?" Charlotte's jaw unhinged as she stared at the awful smirking man.

"I did not imply anything. I stated it. And I'm not waiting for you to finish. I allowed you the option to take a bath first, but I'm done with this nonsense." In one of the quickest movements Charlotte had ever seen, he tugged on the back of his shirt, pulling it off in one yank.

Charlotte turned her back away before she could see anything. She listened intently as he stood, and she could only assume he was divesting himself of his britches.

"Ahh, playing the shy virgin, I see." Although she couldn't see him, she heard the sneer in his voice. "Don't think to try to escape. I'll catch you."

With her back turned, Charlotte tracked his footfalls as he made his way to the tub. She shivered at the sound of water sloshing as he lowered himself into the steaming water.

Charlotte was mortified as she listened to him whistle while moving about the water. The tears she'd been holding back silently tracked down her cheeks. She had been kidnapped by the most dishonorable man she'd ever met. He made Alexander seem as though he was an attentive brother.

After what felt like hours, he pushed himself out of the bath. Charlotte assumed by the noises he was making that he was drying off with a towel that one of the twins had set out.

"Your turn."

Charlotte gasped, not realizing he'd snuck up behind her. With a jerk, he began unlacing her dress.

"Stop. What are you doing?" Charlotte screeched, trying to get away as he continued to undress her.

"I'm getting you clean so I can eat and go to bed. Either I undress you and dump you in that water or you do it yourself."

Charlotte stiffened. Surely, he wouldn't undress her and toss her into the water. He had to be joking. With another tug that had her dress sagging, only held up by her clutching hands, she realized he was not joking.

"Fine, I'll get in the water. You have to turn around."

He let go of her clothing and she felt him step back from her. The removal of his body heat had her skin breaking out in gooseflesh.

"Fine. But hurry. I'm tired."

Charlotte hurried to the tub, glancing back at him to ensure his back was turned. She gasped when he dropped the towel to pull on another set of breeches he pulled from his sack.

Heat rushed up her spine at the sight of his tan body bare in front of her. His rounded rump was white as her untouched skin. The sight of his naked back had heat pooling in her lower belly, a confusing feeling when she hated the sight of him. After moving her focus from his rear, she then noticed the thick crisscrossed pattern of scars running up his back. He stiffened as she gasped again.

"If I'm not allowed to look at you with your clothes off, I feel the same should be said with you. Unless you'd like me to turn around? I can guarantee the front is a much better view."

Charlotte huffed out a shaky breath as she turned her back to him. She undressed quickly and jumped in the water. The warmth of the water was barely holding on. She shivered as she washed herself with quick movements, dunking her head to wash her hair out. After what had to be one of the quickest baths she'd ever taken, she drove toward the towel, wrapped it around her, and moved closer to the fire.

He had kept his word, his back toward her the whole time as he ate in silence.

"Here," he said, tossing her the sack he'd packed when he took her that morning.

Charlotte looked inside and was shocked at how much he had stuffed in the small bag. There were three simple morning dresses and a night rail with a wrapper. Charlotte threw on the night rail and wrapper as fast as she could and snatched a blanket off the bed that she wrapped tightly around her.

"Are you done?" he asked, his voice rough as if he were gritting his teeth.

"Yes," she answered, eyeing his now clothed back.

"Good, come eat so I can get to sleep."

"I'm not hungry," she declared just as her stomach let out a loud rumble as the smell of the stew hit her nose.

"I know you have a hard time telling the truth, but can you stop with the lying at least for the rest of the night? I'm exhausted. Come eat or I'll be forced to stuff food down your damn throat."

Charlotte's spine stiffened. She could tell by the set of his shoulders that he would do just that if she didn't comply with his order. With as much dignity as she could muster, she marched over to the table and sat down with a haughty air that even her aunt would have been proud of.

She took the first spoonful of the thick stew. It was delicious and she lost all semblance of haughtiness as she leaned over the bowl and didn't stop until she was scraping the bottom, ensuring she got every last bite.

"Are you done, or would you like to lick the remnants that you couldn't scrape with your spoon?"

Charlotte dropped the spoon in the empty bowl, appalled at what she'd just done, now that her stomach was full and her sanity was restored. Being in his presence for less than a day and she was losing all the manners she'd been forced to learn.

"I'm done." Charlotte stood and walked over to the bed. Now that her stomach was full, sleep was tugging at her with an unyielding embrace.

He took the empty tray and set it outside. He dumped the water out the window and hung the tub back on the wall where it belonged.

Charlotte struggled to keep her eyelids open. She didn't think she'd ever been as tired as she was at that moment. She hadn't slept well the night before, thinking of all the ways to escape her wedding. She almost laughed, realizing this scenario was not anything she'd come close to imagining the night before. As taxing as it had been, she hadn't slept when she was tucked in the abominable blanket, being jostled by the horse, and she knew she wouldn't be able to think of an escape plan until she was well rested.

"Scoot over," he said as he loomed over her, standing next to the bed.

"What?"

"Get over on the other side of the bed unless you want me to lie on top of you."

"You aren't planning on sleeping in the bed with me, are you?" Charlotte asked, pulling the blankets higher on her body, her eyelids no longer heavy.

He sighed as he pushed her over. Charlotte scrambled out of the bed, but he caught her and hauled her back in.

"I don't have the energy for this."

He climbed into bed next to her with his hand wrapped tightly around her forearm. "Go to sleep. Because of your stubbornness, we won't get much sleep as it is before we have to leave."

He closed his eyes and although he seemed to relax into the mattress, his hold didn't relent. Charlotte watched him in horror as he appeared to be asleep. When his mouth opened and he let out a gentle snore, she attempted to get her arm free. His eyes flashed open in the darkened room, and she pulled back, still unable to get out of his grasp.

"Go to sleep. You'll not be escaping."

With that, he tightened his hold and went back to his soft snores. Charlotte watched him until the sound of his breathing and her own exhaustion pulled her under, and she fell fast asleep still in his hold.

Chapter Three

Charlotte woke up groggy and confused. Her body was plastered against something hard and warm. Charlotte's hand moved across the blanket with a hardness underneath. A soft groan escaping the blanket made her shoot up from her sleeping position, her hand plastered against her apprehender's chest.

"Why, Pet, I didn't know you were so frisky in the morning. Please continue."

Charlotte snatched her hand off him, but he was faster and placed her hand back on his clothed chest. "Let me go," she hissed.

"There she is. My little menace is a shrew in the morning, afternoon, and night. At least you're consistent."

She resisted the urge to slap the smug smile off his face. His eyes were still shadowed by the black cloth he had wrapped around his head.

"I see that you are consistent as well. A scoundrel through and through."

He chuckled, his white teeth flashing, but he stopped before sound could hit her ears.

Charlotte climbed out of the bed and went to the sack where her clothes were stuffed.

"No dress this morning, Pet."

She turned to see he'd also got up and was scrounging through his bag. "Here, Pet, put these on."

He tossed her clothing that she allowed to hit her chest, and she let them fall to the floor. Charlotte watched as he took a deep breath, his hands clenched in and out of a fist.

"We don't have much time. If you don't want me to dress you and throw you back in your blanket prison, I suggest picking those up and putting them on. I'll be back in five minutes. Be ready." He slammed the door and the whole room shook from the force of his anger.

She allowed herself a minute to glare at the door and fight the urge not to put on the clothing he had tossed her, or even better to sneak out and run back home. Charlotte knew she wouldn't get very far, and the thought of traveling in that blanket again made her shudder as her skin crawled.

She picked up the clothes and gasped. They were trousers and a shirt. He couldn't possibly think she'd go outside dressed as a male. Not just a male, but some type of dirty street urchin.

She lifted the material to her nose and was relieved it smelled clean like a salty ocean instead of the filth it looked like it was covered in.

Footfalls sounded up the stairs and although she was sure that the five minutes she was allotted weren't up yet, she didn't trust him. After throwing off the night rail and wrapper, she pulled on the trousers and shirt. They were oddly freeing. Her body only had one layer between her skin and the open air. Her breasts, although tiny, swayed as she walked and the fabric brushed against her in a way she'd never felt before.

Before Charlotte could decide if she liked the feeling or not, he barged back into the room. "Good, you're dressed. I didn't want to waste time wrangling you in a blanket. Jackal has the horses ready. Put your hair up in this and keep your face down as we walk."

Once again, an article of clothing Charlotte had never worn before was tossed at her. This time she caught it. It was a knitted hat, and she turned it around as if she'd never seen one before.

"Come on, Pet, we don't have any time. If you don't want me to chop off your hair with a rusty knife, I suggest you start stuffing. Charlotte continued to stare at the hat. With a huff, he came over and gathered her long, dark locks in his rough hand.

An odd sensation surged in her belly at the gentleness he showed her as he secured her mass of hair under the hat. She was disgusted by herself at how easily she forgot his brutish nature with one act of kindness.

"I can't go out like this," she said when his hands moved away, and he studied his handiwork.

"You can and you will. Jackal procured us food that we can eat on the way. Let's go. And not a word or I'll slit your pretty little throat."

She opened her mouth, but the sharp look he skewered her with stopped her. Even with his eyes still covered by the black scarf, Charlotte knew he would slit her throat. A shiver slithered up her spine, inky and thick. With a silent snick, she closed her mouth and nodded. He continued to stare at her, not letting go of the mesmerizing hold he had on her. After eternity slid by in what had to be only minutes, he nodded back.

Charlotte followed closely behind him. The rickety stairs made her feel as if they were protesting in her defense as she continued to keep her silence. She stared at his back, the solid muscle bunching under his shirt with every step. The power that pulsed off him drilled into Charlotte's eyes until it was branded on her brain. She was stuck. This man had her captive and her freedom leaked from her the closer she got to the sticky floor of the inn.

"Keep your head down," he whispered.

Charlotte jerked her head up and brought it back down as the words penetrated her foggy brain. He pulled her brutally back into reality as the last dregs of hope filtered out of her body.

Charlotte wanted to scream, tear out his muscles, feel the sinew as she pulled and plucked them out just as he plucked her out of her existence. It was a pitiful existence, but it was hers, and she may have had little control, but now she had none. She bled the last measly bits of her control out on the splintered staircase.

He led her to the stables where Jackal waited with the horses. The large, massive beasts' breath came out in a billowy gust of smoked air. Charlotte wanted to sink to the mucked ground and wait until the earth welcomed her back into its embrace. When she mounted the horse, it would be over. She huffed out a laugh at her thoughts.

Stupid girl, it had been over for a while.

Her captor whirled around at her outburst, and she glared at him. She allowed all of her hatred for his actions in taking away the minute fragments of control she had on her life. She gathered all the horrible thoughts from the tips of her toes to the top of her head and pressed them into her glare, wanting him to be stamped with them. Wanting him to stumble back from the force of them.

He did none of that. Instead, he grasped her wrist and hauled her the rest of the way toward the horse.

"Up you go," he said in a jovial tone highlighting the three words.

She stiffened when he grasped her waist, and with ease that showed his muscles weren't just for show, he lifted her on the massive beast.

"Ready, Cap'in?" Jackal asked, his eyes briefly landing on Charlotte before sliding off and back to the horrid man behind her.

No, not a man, a demon. There was not a shred of humanity buried in the thing that settled in behind her.

"Let's go, Jackal. I'm ready to get out of here. Are you ready, Pet?" He didn't wait for her to answer, not that she would have. With a kick to the side, the horse burst into action. The soft ground churned as he pushed the beast to its limits, hurtling them to what Charlotte could only assume was the entrance to hell.

Charlotte refused to allow her spine to melt into the heat his body exuded. She was stiff and with a will she didn't even know she possessed, she kept her eyes open, head held high, and back straight. Tears burned a path down her wind-bitten cheeks when the smell of the ocean invaded her nose. She allowed them to fall without wiping away the evidence.

The briny scent smothered her as docks came into her blurry view. A small rowboat bobbed, as if welcoming her aboard. Charlotte wasn't going to politely accept the invitation. Her captor jumped off the horse as if he weren't hovering several feet in the air.

His hands outstretched to her, beckoning her as if she'd willingly accept her sentence to hell.

No, she may have resigned herself to the clutches of the masked captor, but to capitulate would never happen.

They had another stare down. Charlotte fleetingly realized that even though she'd never seen his eyes, she knew exactly what they were conveying. Shrouded in shadow, she assumed the orbs reflected hellfire.

"Once again making me do it the hard way."

How? How did Charlotte once again underestimate his quickness?

Before her eyelids were able to connect in a blink, his hands spanned her waist and pulled her to the ground. Her head spun from the elevation change. They stood there, neither of them moving. His hands sank into her, the feeling surpassing the rough clothing, her skin, her muscle until it was plastered against her soul.

And still they stood.

Charlotte had a thought that maybe he was pulled into her clutches as much as she was in his. She blinked at the absurdity of the thought, and the spell was broken.

“Shall I carry you?” Even though it was posed as a question, Charlotte wasn’t fooled. It was an ultimatum, and either way she was going to end up on the bobbing boat.

Stiffening her spine to the point of pain, Charlotte threw her shoulders straight and walked with grace and poise. This blackguard could go back to the inferno he was forged from.

Her feet crunched on the graveled sand as the man who had taken control from her followed. The heavy weight of his gaze followed her as she made her way closer to another level of hell. She was confused how Jackal had made it to the little boat without her notice.

How long had they been locked in their stare down?

Her captor hopped onto the boat with the balance of a deadly cat. He reached out that damning hand once again.

Charlotte took a dainty step onto the boat. It couldn't be that hard to get on the boat unassisted, she was less than half his weight. The bobbing accepting boat decided it was done being polite and kicked and bucked as if it were a horse being brought to heel. Jackal's eyes widened, and her captor pulled her down. Her posterior collided harshly with the ocean-worn seat. Charlotte refused to acknowledge either man as the oars dug into the murky water.

A speck of something off the horizon slowly came into focus with every pull of the oars. A large ship formed where a smudge had once been. Charlotte's heart beat as if it were moving sludge through her veins.

"Why are you doing this?" she rasped out. Each word felt as if it rode up her throat on a rusty kitchen knife. She hated herself for the show of weakness. She had been quiet since the moment he told her he would slit her throat. How was that only that morning?

Charlotte wondered if she broke her silence because the thought of having her throat slit no longer scared her as it had earlier. With the way her throat ached at the moment, she would eviscerate it herself if she continued to speak.

Neither man answered her.

She wasn't surprised.

The tiny boat knocked against the larger ship. Charlotte hoped it would bang against it over and over again until it was splintered, just like her soul. She would take her chances with the sea life. Once again, her wishes were blown away with the sea breeze.

A ladder skipped down the side of the ship. Jackal grabbed a hold of it and secured the tiny boat to the ship with hooks bigger than Charlotte's hand. Without a word, Jackal made his way up the ladder with more ease than a man his size should.

"Up you go."

Charlotte's gaze was wrenched from Jackal's hulking form, right before he made his way over the side.

"Please let me go." She didn't look at him. Just the bobbing of the side of the small boat. She knew he wouldn't answer, and if he did, she knew what the answer would be.

"You have three seconds before I throw you over my shoulder and climb that ladder. One."

Charlotte grasped the first rung and pulled herself up. She gave Jackal even more credit with the ease with which he had climbed. The ship swayed in the ocean as if it were entranced by a lullaby the sea was singing to it. Charlotte's stomach swayed, but the dance wasn't as hypnotic as the ship's.

Sweat gathered at the base of her neck until it was released by its weight and slid down her spine. When she reached the top of the ladder, two big, beefy arms wrapped onto her wrists and lifted her onto the deck. Jackal released her with a wink.

"You'll be fine, little bird." With another wink, he moved off to the other sailors running around in organized chaos.

An overbearing presence pressed against Charlotte's back. "Keep your eyes down. These are a swarthy lot and having a woman on the ship is bad luck in their eyes."

Some of them looked up but quickly diverted their eyes when the captain barked orders at them.

The name, Captain, made sense to Charlotte now. He was a literal captain of a large ship full of superstitious sailors. Who didn't appear to know how to treat a lady if his words were to be taken truthfully. The captain moved ahead of her, blocking her view from his crew. She followed behind him, not wanting them to look too closely at her disguise.

They were silent. The only sound that ricocheted off Charlotte's eardrums was the bustling ship crew and her steps. How could someone so large be so quiet?

“Here we are.” With a flourish, the captain opened the door to a large stateroom. The smell of sea and man assaulted her nose. She tried to hold her breath, but his scent coated her nose and painted her blood vessels until it pumped through her with every heartbeat. Charlotte was absolutely certain she was in his room.

“Please, please let me go.” She tried one more time.

He ignored her, ushering her into the room.

“I have to go up to the deck. Can I trust you not to smash every one of my personal belongings?”

Before he could finish his sentence, Charlotte grasped the first thing she could and hurtled it at his face. He batted it away as if she were an annoying nuisance. Charlotte refused to acknowledge that he had almost plucked the thought of destroying everything in his room from her mind as if it were open to his perusal.

He sighed as if she were the one making his life hard. “Always doing it the hard way.”

With one hand, he captured both of hers and dragged her to the bed. A stretch of rope was knotted tightly to a post. The other was already knotted and waiting for its captor. Charlotte kicked and bit the five steps it took to get to the rope.

"Enough. Although I am the captain of this ship and the men are under my order, it doesn't mean that a mutiny isn't possible. You will be safe here as long as they don't know you're here. The moment they know I have brought a woman aboard, they are either going to throw you overboard so as not to have bad luck, or throw your skirt over your head and use you as a port doxy." He ticked his head to the side as he secured the rope. "Or both, and I wouldn't be surprised if it wasn't in that order. So shut your mouth and rest. As long as you're in here, you'll be safe."

He walked away and thought better of it, turning sharply on his silent feet, and stuffed a handkerchief in her mouth. "Don't get any ideas. Jackal is right outside the door, and he has been ordered to knock you unconscious if you decide not to heed my warning."

And then he was gone. Charlotte stared at the heavy wooden door, not knowing what she was waiting for. Her mouth went dry, the cloth soaking up all the saliva her body could produce.

Chapter Four

Charlotte thrashed against the rope. The fibers bit into her, gnawing against the delicate skin of her wrist. The pain pushed the last remnants of rational thought out of her mind. Any shred of sanity leaked away with the blood that ran down her arm. The red rivulet caught her eye and slammed her back into reality.

Charlotte dragged in a frantic breath, and then another slower, deeper. And then she did it again. Forcing herself to calm. She'd been out of control her whole life. And her whole life had been out of her control.

She decided, no more.

Agatha had faith that she was strong even if Charlotte didn't believe it. This time she was going to put her faith in Agatha's belief. She'd never seen the old woman proven wrong before, and she hoped it wouldn't start with her.

She'd been kidnapped, forced to spend a night with said kidnapper, and now she was on his ship, bound by a salt-drenched rope. What her kidnapper didn't know about her was that she wasn't as helpless as she appeared. She practiced knots long after Jack had abandoned her all those years ago.

Charlotte scoffed at herself as she wished she could blow a stray lock of hair out of her face. How had she let her life get so far away from her? She internally went into herself and saw what others had seen, what she had even allowed herself to believe, and she hated it.

Something metallic rushed through her veins. It was thick and felt as if she were transforming from the inside. Charlotte stared at the blood running down her arms. She took in the raw marks marring her perfect skin and had a sick satisfaction from the imperfection. She was done allowing others to shape how she saw herself. She no longer cared what people thought of her. In a way, she hoped they would still see her as a weak girl who allowed others to choose her life for her.

Being underestimated was never a bad thing.

Charlotte studied the knot as a sly smile crept on her face. Using the blood as a macabre motivator, she focused on her way to freedom. Charlotte methodically worked the gag out of her mouth using her tongue until it ached, when she finally spat the offending cloth out, she bared her teeth and began picking apart the knot. Sweat beaded on her forehead, her concentration breaking when she had to blink the raw sting away. Time crept by unnoticed as she continued working. The knot slowly unraveled, and a sly smile graced her lips as she gained more and more of her freedom.

This was the new Charlotte, and even though she'd only just stepped into the new role, she was already enjoying the resourcefulness she was showing. Not bothering to rub the abraded skin, unsure how long she had before her captor came back, Charlotte sprinted toward the heavy wooden door.

She wrenched the door open and ran face first into her captor.

She'd been so close.

So close.

Tears prickled the back of her eyes, and her throat closed, but Charlotte refused to show the dejected emotion pushing through her. This was just her first attempt. She would succeed next time.

"Going somewhere, Pet?"

She glared up at him, defiance pulsing from her eyes. She was not going to give him any more entertainment.

With a firm hand, he pushed her back into the room and closed the door that had been her freedom not seconds before.

"Let me go." Charlotte was proud of how calm her voice sounded. Even with her throat clogged with unshed tears, burning as she pushed them down, she still sounded under control.

"Ahh, I can't do that. We have left the harbor and are now in open seas."

Her body jerked to get away from his touch but more so because she hadn't even realized the ship was no longer land bound. She had been so caught up in her escape that the outside noises hadn't registered.

She now felt the rocking of the ship, which was no longer the gentle movement as they were anchored in the harbor. The rocking was more pronounced as if the ocean were welcoming the ship back with hearty slaps.

"What did you expect to do when you made it up on the deck?" he asked as he plopped down on the chair that was tucked under the desk. His nonchalance infuriated her.

"I was going to get as far away from you and your crew. I was never going to think about you again as I started my life the way I want to live it." Charlotte snarled, anger surging through her as the reality of her first escape attempt was ruined.

Damn this infernal man. She was so close.

"Pet, you do understand you are on a ship with a crew of unruly pirates. I don't know what you expected by leaving my quarters, but having you show up on deck would have caused a mutiny."

"Pirate ship?"

"Really, Pet? Out of everything I've said, that was what your tiny mind latched onto."

"I do not have a tiny mind." Charlotte seethed. And learning she was on a pirate ship was pertinent information.

"Once again, you are grasping the wrong things I'm saying to you."

He sat back, making the wooden chair creak in protest. He rubbed the bridge of his nose as if he were exasperated with her and not the other way around. "I'm going to say this once since you insist that you do not have a tiny mind, so please pay attention."

The scathing annoyance in his voice put Charlotte's back teeth on edge. She wanted to scratch and claw the smug look off his shadowed face. How was it the more time she'd spent with this infuriating man the more she despised him?

"You are aboard the illustrious ship, Persephone. And I, my dear Pet, as I'm sure with your astuteness can ascertain that I'm—"

"Hades." Charlotte's face felt cold as all the blood drained from her cheeks. A low buzzing overtook her eardrums.

He stood, his large, tall frame engulfing her with his mere presence. He gave her a small, disrespectful bow. "At your service." A shock of white teeth appeared through his beard, reminiscent of a lion she'd once seen at the zoological gardens.

Even in her sheltered existence, she'd heard of the notorious pirate Hades. He was sought after by the crown as it was rumored he was running weapons and other supplies to the colonies to help in their war effort.

Her legs shook, but she refused to show him weakness. Locking her legs together to stop their trembling, she cleared her throat, hoping the knocking in her knees was only discernible to her ears.

"Ah, you've heard of me." His teeth continued to show as his smile grew. "Convenient. I don't have to explain to you how deadly of a situation you're currently in. I'm not sure if you've heard my earlier statement that women on boats are bad luck, but it is a superstition among sailors, and my men are a superstitious lot. If they saw you like I've warned you before, they'd either want to throw you overboard or throw your skirts up. Heed my warning this time, Pet."

"You're telling me you have no control over your crew? I guess the rumors of your terrifying demeanor were grossly exaggerated. And as you are aware, I'm not wearing a skirt."

Charlotte ran her hands down the front of the trousers, which she loathed to admit were more comfortable than she'd expected. Also, more convenient. He tracked the movement of her hands and even though she was still unable to see what was under that damned scarf, she felt as if he were undressing her with his hidden eyes.

"Pet, in that statement, you are correct. I am very aware you are not wearing a skirt. Your arse in those infernal trousers has had me at a cock-stand all day. As for my reputation, there are others I could be persuaded to prove to you are true."

Charlotte inhaled deeply at his crude words. She was confused as to the flare of heat that pulsed through her veins at the mention of his nether regions.

"Well, you and your..." She cleared her throat but refused to back down. This was the new Charlotte, she reminded herself. "Cock-stand can go to the devil."

He chuckled darkly and another flare pulsed through her. "Pet, don't you remember I am the devil. And even the devil seems to want to protect you from the heathens upstairs. At the moment, you're only good for one thing to anyone on deck. I suggest staying here where the temptation is contained. Yes, all my men are petrified of me, but with an arse like that, some may feel torture and death are worth it. I'm ensuring none of my men ruin you more than you already are."

No longer were Charlotte's cheeks cold. They flamed at his words, and it wasn't for what he thought it was. Hot and thick anger pushed all fear of the dreaded Hades away.

"I assure you I'm good for more than one thing. In fact"—she gestured to the apex between her legs—"I'm sick of this being the only thing of value on me. I promise you." She took a step closer to him, seething with the knowledge that because of what was between her legs she was seen as useful for one thing. Less than.

Her cunny seemed to be a bargaining chip for everyone but herself. Her brother used it to get the estate out of debt, and now she was here, told to be a good little captive or she'd be divested of the only thing of worth these men recognized.

A dastardly thought rushed through her head, and instead of dismissing the insanity of it, she allowed it to grow until it took over all her rational thought.

She held her ground, staring at the shadowed darkness of his eyes. "I promise you, Hades." She put all her hatred and revulsion for him, of her, of her situation in the forming of his name on her lips. "Nobody on your crew could ruin me. They could try, like so many others have before, but they will not succeed." By the end of her tirade, Charlotte's words were hissed out of her.

He stepped closer. The toes of their boots knocked together. Both were breathing at an uneven pace.

"You're not listening to what I'm saying," he stated, his words coming out in a low rumble.

"No, I don't think you're listening to what I'm saying. In fact, let me go up there or send one of your men down here. Send six. I'm done letting others dictate my life through my body."

A deep, dark sound pushed out between his teeth. Charlotte shivered at the ominous sound, but she held her ground.

"Send anyone down here, huh? You don't care who defiles you as long as you have an alibi?"

Charlotte was confused by his question. Why on earth would she need an alibi? It wasn't as if she asked to be kidnapped. His nearness was making her lightheaded. As they breathed in each other's labored exhales, all lucid thoughts scrambled in her mind.

"Yes." She wasn't sure what she just agreed to. She needed him to leave, move. She couldn't clear her head with him so close.

“Let’s get one thing straight, Pet. Nobody else is touching you. On this ship or on this earth. From now to eternity.”

With his uttered oath, his lips slammed down on hers. Charlotte sucked in a shocked breath. Confusion and something she couldn’t identify wrapped around her. This turn of events was not what she had in mind, but as his firm lips coerced hers into submission, Charlotte didn’t understand why she wasn’t pushing him away.

Her fingers curled into the soft fabric of his shirt, anchoring him to her, or maybe it was the opposite, and she was anchoring herself to him.

His warm hand caressed the back of her neck as his fingers stroked the sensitive skin.

Charlotte had never been kissed. Living in the country, attending her ailing father had stopped her from having any type of season. Her brother only came home on rare occasions and never brought anyone with him. She’d known she was uneducated in the art of seduction, but this kiss couldn’t have been a normal occurrence among debutantes.

Charlotte’s knees gave way when he sucked her bottom lip into his mouth, tracing it with his tongue. His other hand wrapped around her waist, bringing her flush against him. His hold was the only thing keeping her upright.

His tongue tantalized her into opening her mouth where it slowly invaded the silky depths. Her eyes snapped open at the intrusion, and she cursed when she noted the scarf was firmly in place, hiding his eyes from hers.

Charlotte felt languid as his tongue caressed hers. Coaxing hers to explore as his was. With shy curiosity, Charlotte allowed herself to be educated in this forbidden art she'd never been exposed to before.

He moaned into her mouth as she copied the movements he was teaching her. She clung to him, allowing her muscles to give up any semblance of doing their job. His hand slid down her waist, and fire burned where his fingers branded into her clothed skin.

She pressed her aching breasts against his chest. The heat of his skin caused her nipples to harden and prickle from the pressure. A groan escaped him and marked his eagerness, an ancient language that Charlotte wasn't even aware she understood. She moaned back, answering his plea of pleasure.

Cool air hit her heated thighs as the too large trousers trailed down her legs, landing with a thud that she couldn't hear from the pounding in her ears. Her head tipped back when his thick fingers ran over her wet cunny. She'd never felt anything as decadent as his palm cupping her most intimate area.

"Oh," she cried when he inserted his blunt finger where nobody had ever touched.

He growled low and guttural as she clenched around him. His mouth traveled down her exposed throat. His lips and tongue licked and sucked as he slowly pushed in and out of her sopping cunny.

Something foreign and terrifying built low and deep in Charlotte's belly. As he continued pushing his finger inside, he tilted her head back, taking possession of her mouth. When his thumb brushed over her pulsing bundle of nerves, Charlotte's body ignited.

She screamed in his mouth as tiny explosions lit throughout her whole body. Charlotte clenched and pulsed around his finger as his thumb slowly slid away from her throbbing clitoris.

He slid his finger out of her and sucked her tongue into his mouth as the blunt head of his cock positioned itself at her entrance. It took Charlotte a second too late to break from the haze she was in, from what had happened to grasp the enormity of what was about to occur.

"Wait," she cried just when he thrust inside of her.

Pain lanced through her, causing her muscles that were languid mere seconds ago to tense. She'd heard the maids whispering about the pain from having one's maidenhead breached, but she hadn't expected such pain right after experiencing something so blissful.

Hades stilled. His muscles might have been tighter than hers.

His lips slid from hers as did his cock. Even though she couldn't see his eyes, she could see the shock on his face without having access to his eyes. He grasped her shoulders and held her away from him.

"Bloody hell, you're a virgin?" he rasped, the shock still staining his face.

Charlotte looked down at the impressive cock that had impaled her. The tip smeared with red. Her blood, she realized.

"I was," she answered.

Chapter Five

It was done. She was no longer a virgin. No longer would it be held over her head as a threat. She was in control of herself from now on. She refused to acknowledge her cry to stop right before he pushed inside of her. That was a momentary lapse of reason that didn't change the outcome in the least.

It happened, and now it was done.

His mouth snapped shut. The sound of his teeth clacking together echoed through the quiet room. His fingers flexed on her shoulders before he snatched them away from her as if she'd burned him.

He glanced down, his erection gone but the blood still prominent on his large cock even in its flaccid state. He jerked his pants up without looking her in the face.

He pushed past her and yanked the door open. "Do not leave this room, Charlotte."

She startled, hearing her name from his lips for the first time. His voice was low and menacing as if she were the one who'd wronged him.

Not waiting for an answer, he slammed the door behind his retreating back. She listened as his feet pounded up the stairs until the only thing she could hear was her own sharp breathing.

The door blurred in a distorted vision. Only when Charlotte blinked did she notice she was crying and the door wasn't warping in front of her eyes. Large, silent tears spilled over her lids, trickling down her chilled cheeks. She wouldn't have been shocked if they froze on their journey as she didn't think she'd ever be warm again.

She'd played with fire and instead of being burned, as she was warned by Cook many times when she would sneak into the kitchen, no, she wasn't burned, not even singed; she was frozen. He did exactly what she wanted. He divested her of the burdensome virginity. If she was being honest with herself, he actually made it somewhat enjoyable. Or at least his fingers did.

What had she been thinking?

What little warmth she'd been hording seeped out of her. She flexed her toes, the joints popping loudly as if there were ice chips flowing through her.

How had she gotten so carried away?

He truly had to be the devil. It was the only explanation she could think of that made her feel better about her actions.

Wet, salty droplets of sorrow landed on her chest, but she lacked the energy to remove them. Her whole body ached, even her soul or what little soul she had left as she was certain Hades had siphoned most of it out of her felt bruised. With jerky movements as if her body were no longer under her brain's control, Charlotte sank down to the smooth wooden surface.

Hugging her knees to her chest, she fought to keep herself from transitioning into a statue formed of ice and a partial soul right there on the floor of the notorious pirate ship Persephone.

Charlotte wasn't sure how long she sat on the unforgiving floor. The ship rocked her stiff body as if to soothe her, yet she was past being soothed. There was no going back to her life after she had allowed Hades to ravage her. Not that she wanted to go back to the miserable existence she'd been living, but no longer having the option was terrifying.

A hesitant knock landed on the still blurred door. Charlotte blinked, bringing the large wooden door into focus. She held her breath, unsure of what to do. The knock came again before the door hesitantly opened.

A small boy with large golden eyes and a mop of golden hair peeked around the frame.

“’Ello, my lady. The captain asked me to bring you a hot bath. Are you all right, my lady?” He blinked at her with confusion, creasing his little forehead as he studied her on the ground.

Charlotte smiled, surprised when her frozen cheeks didn’t crack from the duplicity of the action. “I’m perfect.” Her voice was as chilled as the rest of her, and she didn’t recognize the sound as her own. “I was just sitting on the ground, getting my sea legs.”

He cocked his head as if she needed to be sent to bedlam. Charlotte stifled a giggle as she pictured what she must look like to the poor young boy. She most likely looked like the perfect picture for bedlam.

“I find that if you take deep breaths and move with the ship, your body gets used to the rocking. I’ve never seen anyone sit on the ground.”

As if she aged fifty years since the captain stormed out, Charlotte’s body protested as she pushed to her feet. Her vision went black on the sides and slowly crawled toward the middle of her sight. She blinked furiously, refusing to shed another tear. What was done was done.

She swayed and had to reach out and hold on to the wall to keep herself steady. "I don't think my way worked. Maybe I'll try your way next."

The small boy grinned as if she were the most entertaining thing he'd witnessed, which would be saying something since he was on a boat with pirates.

"Aye, I think you should try it my way." He gave her a solemn look as if he were the adult with the answers and she were the newborn figuring out life.

Maybe that description was more apt than any outside observer would have guessed.

"Would yah?"

Charlotte blinked, wondering if she'd momentarily blacked out and missed out on an important conversation.

"Would I, what?"

He let out an exasperated sigh, but then he straightened as if he remembered who he was talking to. "Would you like a hot bath?"

"Oh." Charlotte would have blushed if she had any heat within her to coat her cheeks. "Yes, I would very much like a hot bath."

The boy studied her for a moment longer as if waiting for her to do something else that made no sense to him. When she stared at him without so much as twitching, he must have determined the entertainment was over and moved farther into the quarters.

He pulled a large tub out from a hidden compartment and began carrying buckets of steaming water.

"Can I help you?" Charlotte asked as his slight shoulders hunched when he hefted yet another bucket.

He glanced at her as if she once again said something silly and foreign. "No, my lady."

Charlotte sat on the bed after he'd bumped into the desk for the second time as he tried to move the buckets through the room with her standing lamely in the middle of it.

When the tub was full of steaming water, the boy went about getting out a bar of lovely smelling soap and a rag. "Is there anything else you need?" he asked, glancing up at the ceiling.

Charlotte recognized the look of longing on his face. She suspected he wanted to be up on the deck in the fray instead of lugging buckets of water for some odd lady's bath.

"Yes, one more thing."

The boy's shoulders slumped before he pulled them back and glanced at her. "What can I do for you, my lady?"

"What's your name?"

His golden eyes went blank for a second as if he couldn't comprehend her question. "Cerberus."

Charlotte blinked and this time her face went blank at the name she had not been expecting. "It is nice to meet you, Cerberus. You may call me Charlotte."

He bobbed his head once again and his golden eyes strayed to the ceiling. "Thank you for my bath, Cerberus. I think I can manage from here."

"Thank you, my lady. I mean, Charlotte." With a hasty bob, he rushed out of the room as if his namesake were on his heels.

Charlotte made sure the door was shut firmly before stripping out of her clothing and almost sprinted to the heated tub. She hissed as the hot water burned her frozen body. Her skin stung as if she were burning in hell as she sank quickly in the water. Tears pricked her eyes as her body acclimated to the water and its no longer frozen state.

Charlotte scrubbed her body over and over again until the bar of soap was half the size it had been when she started, and her body was red and raw from the repeated washing.

When the water lost its last vestige of warmth, she scrambled out of the tub, worried her skin would go back to its chilled state and shed the heat she had absorbed. She picked up her clothing with disgust, hating the thought of having to put the filthy clothes on her abraded skin.

She sniffed the offending clothing and dropped it to the ground. Without a hint of guilt, Charlotte threw open the trunk at the bottom of the bed and pulled out a large, clean shirt. The material was worn and soft against her body. It was so large one of her shoulders peeked out from the collar and it went well past her knees.

With nothing else to do, Charlotte plodded to the bed. With every step, her muscles lost another ounce of strength. She barely had the capacity to pull the heavy blanket over her shoulder before sleep claimed her.

Chapter Six

A loud snore woke Charlotte out of her deep sleep. Even with the sound of Hades snoring, she cracked her eyes open, afraid the breeze of her eyelashes would wake the sleeping beast. From the low lamplight, Charlotte studied the sleeping man and hatred bubbled through her.

How dare he sleep in the same room as her.

Yet, he once again underestimated her.

Good.

He allowed himself to be vulnerable without restraining her as if he hadn't a fear in the world with her sequestered in his room. Charlotte spied the lethal letter opener in a holder affixed to his desk. The gold handle glinted in the lamplight as if beckoning her with its potential sin.

Holding her breath, Charlotte slunk out of the heavy blanket without making a whisper of a sound. Her eyes widened from the shock of cold that assaulted her feet when they quietly connected to the wooden floor. But she was steadfast in her silent mission.

The letter opener weighed heavily in her palm as she held the handle, allowing her heat to soak into the weapon. The insufferable man continued to snore, without a care in the world. His scarf wasn't gracing his head and Charlotte took in the thick black hair that curled around his ears, too long to be fashionable but fit him perfectly. His nose twitched and she jolted, staring at his closed eyelids, begging them to stay that way. And they did. He slept with the ease of someone who had no burdens. As if he hadn't kidnapped a woman on her wedding day, threatened her numerous times, kissed her as if it were his one purpose in life, took her virginity, abandoned her, and sent her a hot bath.

Charlotte took a steadying breath through her nose.

Quick and hard. She repeated in her head as she pictured repetitively thrusting the weapon into his cold, dead heart.

She despised that her hand shook as she lifted her makeshift weapon and let it hover over his heart. She took another deep breath, deciding she would push on the count of three.

One.

Two.

Th—

A large, calloused hand engulfed her smaller, delicate one, digging the letter opener into her palm. Charlotte's eyes shot up to see him staring at her in the lamplight. His eyes were dark, but she couldn't make out the exact shade in the dim light, but even without the light, she knew he was locked onto her face.

"You're too high, Pet." His voice was low as if he didn't want to break the spell of the moment.

Charlotte's throat closed, making breathing almost impossible and stopping speech altogether.

"If you want the heart, you need to go lower. In between the ribs and thrust up. Thrust up, hard." Still holding her hand, he moved the weapon lower, pressing the tip of the opener a thumbprint lower than where she had first aimed. He pushed the tip firmly into his chest until a dark liquid seeped into his pristine white shirt.

"Why are you doing this?" Charlotte asked, mesmerized as the blood bloomed onto his shirt.

"Ahh, Pet. I feel I owe you. I spilled your blood, it's only fair I allow you to spill mine."

With deliberate timing, Charlotte allowed her gaze to leave the hypnotic sight of his shirt soaking up the blood they had spilled together to settle on his lamp-lit eyes.

"Come on, Pet. I put you exactly where you need to be to exact your revenge for taking your maidenhead without your permission. You could collect the reward the throne has issued for the capture of the dreaded pirate Hades. All you have to do is push, and you will never have to worry about money or someone making decisions for you again."

It struck Charlotte at that moment he wasn't sleeping next to her because he thought she was harmless. He knew she was going to attempt to kill him, and he had given her the chance to do so.

"I let you."

One of his eyebrows rose. They were thick and black, the sharp arch making him look even more formidable.

"I let you take my virginity." She answered his unasked question. "I taunted you, hoping you'd rid me of my maidenhead. Having that held over my head was getting cumbersome and you were as good as any to divest me of it. That act is not the reason why I want to kill you," Charlotte whispered as if she were confessing something sacred.

He swallowed. The shadow of his Adam's apple bobbed in the flickering lamplight. His eyes bounced back and forth from her face back to her eyes like he was trying to read something on her face that she hadn't spoken out loud.

Charlotte let him memorize her face, not knowing what he would see but oddly hoping he found it.

“I was sick of people hanging it over my head. The constant threat of bodily harm becomes tedious as a woman. Now it has been eliminated on my own terms. And honestly, I cannot see why it causes such an uproar.”

He blinked at her as if processing what she’d just admitted. Charlotte jolted when he threw his head back and laughed, a harsh sound as if it wasn’t something he did often. “Pet, you wound me. You seemed to enjoy my fingers.”

Charlotte pressed the letter opener a fraction deeper, hoping to distract him from his embarrassing words. His smile widened as more blood was absorbed into the thirsty fabric of his shirt.

“Well.” She cleared her throat from the uncomfortable tightness. “I did enjoy that part. It was the part that is so scandalous that has me flummoxed.”

“If you hadn’t sweetly expressed you weren’t particular on who divested you of your virginity, I promise, Pet, it would have lasted much longer, and you would have the full comprehension of what has all the old biddys of the ton in a tizzy.”

“All I hear is excuses.”

Once again, he laughed, the sound not as rusty as the first time. "Once again, you wound me, Pet."

She glanced down at the letter opener still causing small droplets of blood to seep into his shirt. "Yes, I can see that. Don't fret. I think you'll live."

"Now answer me, Pet. If not for soiling your reputation beyond redemption, why did you take advantage of my vulnerable form with the sharpest thing in my cabin?"

So, she was correct. He had laid out a trap, allowing her to seek her revenge. This man was an enigma. An enigma she needed to keep her guard up with. He seemed to always be steps ahead of her and she refused to trust this placating pirate.

"Because, as I mentioned, I am sick of everyone running my life for me. If it wasn't my father, it was my brother, and now you. I think it is time for me to start living the way I want, with my opinion being the only one I will take counsel with."

"And killing me would help you in your cause?"

"I had to start somewhere. And as you have mentioned, you are the pirate Hades, traitor to the crown. I was unaware of the hefty reward. Thank you for that tidbit of knowledge."

"Always your faithful servant."

"Why? Why would you go against your home?"

He watched her once again. Charlotte thought he was searching for something on her face.

"I'll answer your question if you answer one of mine."

Charlotte jiggled the letter opener against his seeping chest, reminding him that he wasn't in the position to ask for anything. Yet, she hated to admit that she was enjoying this interaction with him. He was talking to her and giving her the respect she never realized she'd craved.

"If you were going to kill me, you would have done it already. Either before I taught you where to thrust or immediately after."

"Ask your question, Pirate." Charlotte infused steel in her voice, refusing to lose the upper hand even if it was just an illusion.

"If not for being ruined, why were you marrying that wrinkled old ball sack, who if rumor is right, was the reason the last two of his wives met their untimely demise."

"Ruined?"

This hadn't been the first time he'd alluded to her not being chaste. His reaction when he breached her maidenhead was enough proof that she hadn't been wrong with the implications.

It was his turn to clear his throat. She watched the strong muscles of his neck and had the strangest urge to run her tongue up the ridged line.

"I could only think of one reason for someone such as yourself to willingly marry a man who could be your grandfather and a possible murderer."

"And that would be?" Charlotte knew what he was going to say, but him squirming under her gaze made her feel powerful and she had come to the conclusion she was going to keep the feeling.

"I assumed, rather foolishly it appears, you had been ruined by some scoundrel and was marrying the man to save face and give him a possible heir, eliminating his murderous tendencies."

"You thought I was with child?" She widened her eyes in shock and raised her voice an octave. Not that she wasn't expecting his answer, but she was certain her surprise would make him even more uncomfortable.

With the way his face paled, she'd been correct. She ruined the façade by allowing the smile she was struggling to contain to grace her face.

"You minx." He chuckled, the movement jostling the letter opener, reminding them both of its presence. "Do you think we could take the weapon off my person?"

Charlotte conceded, moving back until she was sitting on the edge of the bed with her pilfered weapon still in her clutches.

"My brother sold me to him," Charlotte explained, wanting to spit the vile words out and wash them down with a gallon of wine. When he didn't respond, she continued. "After my father died, my brother discovered that the estate was in considerable debt and from what I've inferred, most of it was to the neighboring estate. I wasn't privy to the conversation because why would I be involved in my future? One of the two odious men, my brother or Lord Sterling, decided I would be payment for my father's debt."

"Your brother is aware of how Lord Sterling handles situations involving his wives being unable to produce an heir, is he not?"

She nodded, confused but proud at the absence of tears. Anger at her brother and Lord Sterling, and her father as well if she was adding to the list, infused her blood. She didn't want to weep. She wanted revenge.

New Charlotte was in full metamorphosis, it seemed.

"I'll kill him."

"Which one are you referring to?" she asked, cocking her head at the menace in his declaration.

His beard twitched, making Charlotte wonder how hard he was clenching his back teeth.

"Both," he spat.

"Why? Why do you even care?"

"You asked me why I deliver goods to the colonies. Are you ready for your answer?"

She wasn't stupid, and she refused to be timid. "I would like the answer for both if you'd be so kind."

"I'm not kind, Pet. I'm not obliged to explain the reason why I rescued you from your wedding, but I will grant you the answer as to why I bring supplies to the colonies to assist in their war efforts."

"How honorable of you." She rolled her eyes and attempted to appear uncaring about his answer even though she knew she was going to hang on to his every word.

"It's the same reason you had that damnable letter opener pressed to my chest moments ago. Freedom, Pet. All these people want is freedom to develop the new land they are now living on the way they want to. Why should they have to bow down to a crown that's an ocean away? We all want the freedom to become the person we were meant to be without the restraints of others telling us what to do. It's a pursuit I understand and also crave."

Charlotte opened her mouth and shut it numerous times as she wanted to dispute his statement, but at every turn, she couldn't.

Freedom was a heady dream, and he assisted people in achieving it. A noble cause for the devil himself.

"Why risk it for people you don't even know? As you said, you have a hefty price on your head and if caught, any semblance of freedom you currently have will be stripped away, as will your head from your neck."

He chuckled again and Charlotte found herself warming to the sound. Pride prickled her chest at the knowledge that she was the one pulling the sound out of him.

"What a gruesome picture you paint for me, Pet. It's a good thing I won't get caught."

"It's the ones who think they are invincible that fall the hardest."

He stood, his steps slow and measured, yet it felt as if he stood in front of her in the blink of an eye. "Worried for me, are you?"

He leaned until their foreheads touched. His breath ghosting over her cheeks as his question lingered in between the minute separation between their lips.

“Yes,” she answered. She exaggerated the S at the end, briefly touching her bottom lip to his. Just the minuscule touch of their lips ignited a fire only he could flame.

“I’m worried because I don’t have a way of getting you to England to collect the reward on your head. I refuse to waste all that money. And as you so astutely stated, I am in search of my freedom and I’m going to use you to get it.”

“Devious.”

He gripped the back of her neck and yanked her to his mouth. Charlotte welcomed his tongue, greedy to be surrounded by him. She couldn’t understand why he made her feel powerful, but he did, and she reveled in it.

But only for a moment.

Charlotte positioned the letter opener at the thudding pulse on his neck. He pulled back a fraction. Just enough for their eyes to connect.

He stroked her cheek with his knuckles. “Good, Pet. Don’t let your guard down for anyone.”

“Even you?”

“Especially me. I want to devour you.”

Before she could come up with a retort, there was a loud knock.

He stood, looming over her, his gaze never moving from hers. “What?”

“Captain, we can’t find Cassiopeia.” Cerberus’ fear-soaked voice filtered through the wood.

Hades rubbed the bridge of his nose before inhaling deeply. “Did she eat tonight?”

His eyes still hadn’t moved from hers as he spoke through the door.

“Yes, Captain. Cook made her favorite meal, but she is nowhere to be found.” The whine in the boy’s voice showed how upset he was.

“Well, we can’t have my favorite girl lost, now, can we?”

The little boy’s voice trembled. “No, Captain.”

“Get some sleep. You’ll be safe here.” He kissed her cheek before turning to the door. Without a backward glance, he wrenched the door open to a fear-filled Cerberus. The boy’s eyes were shining as if one blink would cause a tidal wave of tears to rush down his cheeks. The connection between Charlotte and Hades was severed as the door closed behind them, leaving her alone.

Chapter Seven

Charlotte glared at the dense wooden door. The horrid man had another woman aboard the ship. She was once again the old Charlotte, allowing others to lead her through life. She curled up on the bed, wanting to scream. She hadn't made any progress in finding herself. The one Agatha proclaimed she would be. She'd actually allowed him to kiss her. There was no reason for them to be intimate again. He took her virginity as she had planned. She never thought to seek out a repeat performance.

It didn't matter that he spoke to her as if he did care about her opinions. The conversation they had, even with her pressing a letter opener to his chest, was the most adult conversation she'd ever had.

And she stupidly thought he liked her.

She stabbed the pillow with the letter opener, not having any satisfaction when a plume of feathers exploded in the air.

Was she truly so naïve that she thought the person who kidnapped her would be an ally?

She had secretly hoped to form a friendship with him where he'd allow her the freedom he had passionately waxed on about when speaking of the colonies. Now she was uncertain. If she wasn't the only female on board, maybe he had some nefarious plan for them and freedom was only to be granted to the ones across the water.

He had told her he wasn't ready to tell her why he'd kidnapped her. She felt secure, lulled by the letter opener she had held to his neck. Now she realized it was once again a game he was playing with her, allowing her the illusion of power.

She stabbed the pillow repeatedly until the linen was flat and feathers floated throughout the room. She pictured his face with every thrust. When her arm ached and there were no more pillows to destroy, Charlotte collapsed on the bed. She hadn't slept very long before his snoring had woken her and the high of holding him at knife point was waning.

Her eyelids drooped as she collapsed on the feather-strewn bed. She blew a stray feather off her lips and went to sleep, wondering if he was having an adult conversation with Cassiopeia. Which, funny enough, was her childhood horse's name. She didn't think she hated a name more, unless it was Hades himself.

“What happened here, Pet?” An amused voice brought Charlotte back from a deep oblivion.

She blinked, a feather clinging to her eyelash obscuring her vision. When she moved to wipe it away, she noticed her arm was littered with more of the tiny feathers. Her memory sluggishly came back to her stabbing the pillows until her exhaustion overtook her.

Then the memory of why she stabbed the pillow surfaced.

Cassiopeia.

Being left by the most confusing man she’d ever encountered.

“You made a right mess of my quarters.” He spat a feather that had found its way to the tip of his tongue as he continued to stare at her.

Charlotte glared at him, refusing to engage him in any conversation. If he wanted to converse, he could go find his favorite girl.

“Did the pillow say something offensive?”

When she continued to hold her tongue, he smirked at her. “Get up and clean this mess up.”

“I’m sorry.”

"As you should be. Those were my favorite pillows. Now get up and clean up this mess. I'm exhausted as I'm sure you are as we haven't had a full night's sleep in days."

"And whose fault is that?" she asked, her arms crossing over her stomach. She jerked when one of the offending feathers pricked her.

"You're going to blame this on me?"

"Yes, you've ruined everything, and apparently, I'm not the only one you've decided to ruin." She bit the inside of her lips to keep her from revealing more to him. She refused to have him think the reason she annihilated his pillows was because she was jealous.

No, she was incensed and frustrated.

"And who have you met on this ship besides Jackal and his son, Cerberus? Who pray tell have I ruined?"

They moved together in tandem, cleaning up the feathers and stuffing them inside empty pillowcases.

"I'm not discussing this with you," she muttered as she forcefully stuffed a handful of feathers in the sack.

He stopped thrusting the feathers in his hand into the sack he was holding. He stared at her, his dark eyes sparking with frustration.

Good. They could both be frustrated.

“Pet.” The name made the tiny hairs on the back of her neck stand on end. The venom in that one word made her pause.

She pushed her shoulders back and met his gaze. Did he grow? He seemed so much bigger with the sparks in his eyes. She knew it was unwise to push him. Actually, that wasn’t true. She’d fought him the whole way. She wasn’t the meek girl she was when he kidnapped her, even if that was a little over forty-eight hours ago. In that time, she never truly feared for her life, and she wasn’t afraid for her life at that moment either, but she did worry about the punishment. Just a little.

But he wasn’t going to be privy to that information.

He shoved his half-full sack into her hand and sauntered to the desk chair.

“Finish your task. I’m tired.”

Charlotte pretended she didn’t notice as he began loosening his boot laces. She gathered the rest of the feathers and hated she’d let her temper get the best of her. Only because containing the wayward feathers was a huge pain in the arse.

With her back to him, she climbed into the bed, fluffing the lumpy pillow under her head. Her brain was fuzzy, but she was positive she hadn’t slept more than a couple hours before he barged in demanding an explanation. She needed sleep. It would help her clear her head and help her figure out her next move.

Sleep began to claim her. Her limp body felt heavy, and she welcomed the reprieve, that was until he climbed in next to her. She stiffened, the sleep disappearing as his body heat warmed her.

"You're not sleeping until you tell me what happened." His voice was low, but the authority was undeniable.

"How many women do you have on the ship?" She wasn't going to evade his question, but she would get answers as well.

"Pet, I told you having women on the boat is bad luck. Why would..." he trailed off as understanding dawned on him. "You foolish woman. You ruined my favorite pillows for a cat."

Charlotte bristled at the superior tone, but then his words sank in. "A cat?"

"Yes, Cassiopeia is a mouser cat that Cerberus has become rather fond of. She was below deck with a fat, juicy rat in her rather smug mouth."

Charlotte wished she could float away like the wayward feathers had done. "Why am I here? What are you going to do with me?"

Her back was toward him, unable to meet his gaze in the darkened interior. She felt him stiffen behind her. He was silent for so long she assumed he wasn't going to answer her question.

"Setting you free," he answered. His words were so soft she thought she had conjured them in a dream.

She pinched her arm under the heavy blanket. The pain confirmed her wakefulness. "I don't understand."

"I can't explain everything to you, but I promise you'll be free at the end of this journey."

She turned, wishing the crescent moon shining in through the small window gave more light than it did. She wanted to see his face. She wanted to read him. She wanted to break his skull open and study what he was thinking.

He was on his back, his arms under his head, not giving her any more attention than his words.

"I need more than that, Hades. I need some explanation as to why you took me from my only home on my wedding day."

"Charlotte." He said her name as if it were a plea. The quiet slapping of the water was the only other sound breaking into the sanctuary with stray feathers floating about.

"Hades," she countered, sensing his resolve was breaking and she'd have her answer.

"Jack," he whispered quietly.

Charlotte inhaled sharply, a stray feather striking her in the back of her throat. She sat up and coughed with a ferocity that had her fearing her ribs would crack. Hades rushed out of bed and thrust a skein of water into her hand. Charlotte drank the water, still coughing but no longer in fear of bodily harm.

Had she imagined the name falling off his tongue? The word hung in the air like the feathers she'd stirred in her manic coughing fit.

"What did you say?" Her voice sounded harsh, and she wasn't convinced it was all from her coughing.

He inhaled and Charlotte realized after handing her the water he'd moved as far away from her as he could. She could barely make out his large shape in the dim light, but his liquid brown eyes were locked on her.

Eyes she'd memorized when she was a young, lonely girl. How had she not noticed it before?

"Jack?" The word escaped her mouth. She couldn't believe it, but she couldn't deny it.

"Lottie."

Charlotte sprang from the bed, screeching.

No, he didn't get to call her that.

She ran at him, not registering the frigid wood underneath her feet. Her fist connected with this hard chest, making her knuckles crack. She didn't stop; she pummeled his chest as he stood there, allowing her to brand her frustration into his muscles. Tears streamed down her cheeks as she reconciled the man who'd kidnapped her was Jack.

Her Jack.

Charlotte's knuckles hurt as she continued to connect with Jack's body. She was terrified she wouldn't be able to stop until her hands went through his ribcage and slammed into his heart. Large hands wrapped around her fists, stopping her from hurting herself. She knew her attack was more of a nuisance than anything else to him.

Charlotte blinked away the tears since Jack imprisoned her hands. Her breathing was coming out in short gasps and black dots appeared on the fringes of her vision. A bloom of red seeping out of the wound she'd given him earlier made the blackness encroaching on her vision vanish.

Without thought, she removed her hands from his grasp and pulled at the shirt to see the damage the letter opener had done earlier. The quarters were dim, and her vision swam from her unshed tears, but she still saw it.

"Lottie." Jack's voice was full of emotions she wasn't ready to hear.

With the tip of her index finger, she traced the lettering inked into his skin right above his heart and below the wound she'd given him.

He sucked in a sharp breath as she looped her finger over the name again.

Not just any name.

Her name.

Lottie was scripted above his heart in all its inked glory.

"You left."

He pushed her hand against his chest until it was plastered over her name as if her palm could brand the ink further into his skin. Until it was carved into his heart.

"I came back."

"Ten years. You were gone ten years." Anger, hot and sticky, crawled up her vertebrae, inching toward her tongue.

"I killed, Charlotte. I was young too. I didn't know what was going to happen to me if they didn't see reason."

"They would have listened to you. I told them what happened."

With his free hand, he stroked the back of his finger over her cheek. Her skin felt hot and chapped from everything it had been through the last couple of days.

"I had to leave, Lottie. I needed to make something of myself. Killing Mr. Dons sped up the inevitable."

Charlotte jerked out of his grasp, not wanting to be near him. "And you just show up after a decade of silence?"

Before he could answer, snippets of their earlier conversations flitted through her brain. She paced back to him, poking her finger in his chest. "You thought I was pregnant. What was your plan, Jack?"

He glanced down at her finger but didn't dare move it. He swallowed and she dug her finger deeper into his chest, wishing her letter opener were within reach.

"I wasn't thinking, Lottie. When I heard you were getting married, I was sick with jealousy, wanting to turn my ship around and kidnap you."

"You did kidnap me." She rushed toward the bed and retrieved her letter opener, wanting to skin him alive. To give him a minuscule piece of the upheaval he'd put her in.

He pushed his hand through his thick, curly hair. The motion was like a punch to the gut. Charlotte's vision wobbled as Jack, the Jack from her childhood, converged with this man in front of her. Her Jack was now Hades. And they both ran their hands through their hair when they were frustrated.

"Yes, I did turn my ship around and as much as you hate me, I'd do it again and again as many times as needed to keep you safe."

"Safe?" She wanted to scream the word. She wanted the word to break glass with the intensity of it. It came out in a whisper, yet when he flinched, she felt as if maybe it hit its mark and instead of breaking the innocent glass in the room, it broke something inside of him instead.

"Yes, safe. I stayed away, Lottie. I figured it was what was best for you. I had spies who would give me updates when I came into port. You were safe in the country estate with your father. I heard about your exploits with the old healer, Agatha. You made a name for yourself with your healing abilities. When I came into port, I heard you were to be married and even though I knew it was for the best, it felt as if someone stuck a hot poker through my heart."

"You had people spying on me?" The grip on the letter opener tightened. Her bruised knuckles protested, but her anger snapped at the pain to shut up.

"I needed to make sure you were doing well."

"And you didn't think to send word to let me know how you were faring? Jack, I worried endlessly about you. You vanished and my imagination filled in the blanks every night with another horrible fate for you."

He smirked, the white of his teeth flashing through his beard. "You worried about me?"

"Now who's the one who's picking out the least important part of what I'd just said?" Charlotte threw his words from their night at the inn in his face.

"It's the most important part to me." His ridiculous grin was still plastered to his face and Charlotte hated how much she enjoyed the sight.

"Tell me your plan. What were you planning to do with me after you kidnapped me? I'm sick of everybody keeping things a secret from me, especially when it involves me. No more keeping secrets, Jack. I deserve to know everything." Before Jack could answer, she waved her letter opener in the air as if piercing a thought and pinning it there. "And no half-truths. I want everything. I refuse to live my life with misconceptions and misunderstandings that would clear everything up if people were just open and honest with me."

"As you wish. Just know, Lottie, my motives were pure, asinine but pure."

Charlotte motioned the letter opener back and forth between their chests, encouraging him to speak, showing him she recognized he was stalling with the information she would have.

He leaned against the wall as if his muscles refused to support him in his confession. “When I found out you were to be married, I wanted to come and snatch you away. I listened to my spies tell me how you were growing into the woman you were meant to be. Sheltered but strong, and I wished you would find the strength that I knew you had. Wishing you would shake off the shelter and shine as you should.”

Charlotte’s stomach flipped at his confession. This was Jack, her Jack, recognizing that she was no longer the child he left, but the woman she always wished he would see.

“Lottie, you were my first friend. And all I wanted was for you to be happy. You were so young and innocent the night I killed Mr. Dons and I refused to let my presence ruin you.”

“You were the only good thing in my life. I was alone until you came along. I needed you.” Charlotte moved to the desk chair, no longer able to stand. The letter opener clenched in her fist as if it were a toddler’s stuffed toy. It represented security, and she wasn’t sure she’d ever be able to relinquish it.

“I was scared, Lot. I didn’t know where I was going or what I would do. A man on the docks found me. My hands were still shaking from what I’d done. He took me on his ship. He made me his cabin boy, and I worked my way up until he retired and handed the ship over to me."

"Isn't that fantastic? You were having a grand adventure while I was stuck at home with nobody."

"You were ten and two. Did you expect me to take you with me? The constable and Scotland Yard would have been after us. You saw my back. You saw the scars. It wasn't all a grand adventure. And from what I heard, you had some adventures of your own. I heard about how Agatha taught you how to heal. I thought I was doing what was best for you."

"Or was it what you thought was best for me, but really best for you without the guilt?" She knew her reasoning was ridiculous. Her hurt and anger had her verbally punching him. The scars crisscrossing his back flashed through her mind, but she refused to give an inch. For ten years, she wondered what had happened to him, while he was getting updates.

He ran his hand through his hair again, his whiskey-colored eyes locked on hers. "I did feel guilt every day for leaving you, but also, I felt relief that you were safe. I think if you stopped allowing your anger to cloud your judgment, you'd realize there was nothing else I could do except exactly what I did."

"You're right. I'm angry. And I'm tired. My brain feels as if it is pushing against my skull. You're Jack." She pointed the letter opener at him as if he needed verification of his identity.

"This isn't how I wanted this to happen. I didn't want you to find out this way."

"How did you want this to unfold?"

They were going around in circles and Charlotte refused to allow the exhaustion she was fighting to win until she got her answer.

"I was going to kidnap you, get you away from that insufferable Lord Sterling, and reveal my true identity to you when you were ready."

"And what threshold were you going to use to decide when I was ready? Also, I know you're not telling me everything, Jack Hades Bellamy."

He cringed, his gaze bouncing around the room, never landing on her. "I was going to seduce you and claim the child I thought you were carrying as mine. You were always on my mind. I'm named Hades because you made me tell you the story of Hades and Persephone over and over again. My mouser cat is named after your horse. You were never far from my mind."

Chapter Eight

Charlotte had to strain to hear his confession. Even when the words wrapped around her brain, she couldn't comprehend their meaning until she blinked several times. She never registered his pirate's name or his ship's name until that moment, but she also never thought Hades was Jack. Why would she make the connection?

"You were going to seduce me?"

He shook his head, still refusing to move his gaze to her. "I didn't say it was a good plan. You went and ruined it by seducing me first."

Charlotte sucked in a breath at his blunt reminder of what had occurred earlier. Had it really been less than a day since she'd had her momentary slip in judgment?

"What now?" she asked, not sorry in the least she hadn't complied with his plan.

"I'm uncertain of that answer. I promise I will let you go free, Charlotte. I need to deliver my cargo to the colonies, and after I will set you free."

"I'm not going back to my brother's estate. You can't make me. Between my idiot brother, Alexander, and Mary, my unhinged lady's maid, I will be the next one to commit murder on my family's estate." She was certain he wouldn't do something so cruel, but she needed to state her convictions if not for him but for her.

He sat down on the bed with his elbows anchored to his thighs. His head between his hands as if he were too weary to use his neck to hold up his head and his worries. "I would never take you back to him. I promise, Lot, I will fund whatever you want to do and purchase an estate for you to live. You will never have to worry about being taken away. Just please behave as I get this cargo to port." As if fully registering what she had said, he asked, "Mary? I hadn't heard your brother bringing in another woman."

Charlotte's veins burst with fire, remembering Mary and Jack's embrace all those years ago. The catalyst of the event that caused Jack to leave her. "She'll be heartbroken you don't remember her, Hades." Charlotte knew it was petty to call him by his pirate's name when she was angry at him, but she couldn't help it. "She blamed me when you left, you know?"

"Why would she care?"

Charlotte gaped at him after he asked his asinine question. Did he truly not remember his dalliance with cruel, evil Mary?

"Because, Hades, you broke her heart. You were"—Charlotte's heart thumped hard before she spat the word out—"kissing her. She fancied herself in love with you and blamed me for making you abandon her."

"We were kissing and you saw us?" Even though it was posed as a question, Charlotte knew it was a statement.

Charlotte nodded, afraid that if she admitted it, the hurt and betrayal she'd felt all those years ago would resurface.

"Is that the reason you were alone with Mr. Dons?" This time it was posed as a question, but Charlotte was certain he didn't need her to confirm what was already accepted in his expression.

"I wondered what would have made you slip after all of our training and promises to keep you away from him." He stood, catching the pain in her eyes, and thrust his hand through his hair in utter frustration. "You were ten and two." His words were angry. Charlotte wasn't certain if it was with her or himself. "I was too old to look at you in any way but as a protector. As a brother. You must understand at ten and five I was more mature in certain things and you were not experiencing feelings the way I was." He refused to even glance at her as he attempted to plead with her to understand.

"It still hurt. I was in love with you, Jack. You were my everything, and the betrayal." Her throat closed enough she couldn't fit another word through it.

"I was your everything, Lot. Don't think I didn't know that. It was so unfair for you to only have one person to rely on. I was terrified you were going to settle for me because I was all you had in life. Of course you loved me. I was all you had. I knew you were going to grow into a stunning young woman and as much as it burned, I wanted you to find the love of a lifetime because you deserve all the love this world can offer you."

"Settle. How could you think you would have been anything close to settling? Yes, I was young, but it is ten years later, and you are still the only person I had."

"And I treated you cruelly," he snapped as if building an invisible wall between them.

"True, being kidnapped and rolled in a blanket and forced to ride for hours on a horse in said blanket wasn't the best way to get me out from under my brother's control, but it was effective."

"And what happened after." He gestured to the apex of her legs as if Charlotte needed a clue as to what he was referring to.

"That was purely me, wanting to rid myself of something burdensome."

"You said, wait," he growled, refusing the reprieve she offered.

"It's done. It was my choice. Don't take that power from me, Hades. I'm just starting to feel as if my life might become mine. Allow me to have this."

Charlotte's heart reached out to him. He looked as if he were holding the world on his shoulders. She kept her body firmly planted on the chair. Although she didn't blame him for taking her virginity as he seemed to think was his fault, she still wasn't certain how she felt about his other confessions. With only a few hours of sleep in the past couple days draining her, she was unable to think straight. She needed a full night's rest before she pondered exactly what she wanted to do. New Charlotte wasn't going to make rash decisions. No, new Charlotte was going to take a breath and methodically think about her next move and how she wanted to feel about her current situation.

With that muddled thought, Charlotte took the few steps toward the bed and climbed around him until she was pressed against the wall, giving him as much of the bed as possible. He sighed wearily and moved to the chair instead of lying down next to her.

His soft snores sounded before she could decide if she wanted to invite him to share the bed with her. With the sound of his rhythmic breathing, Charlotte succumbed to the wishes of her sleep-deprived brain and fell into a deep sleep where thankfully she didn't dream.

A loud bang thrust Charlotte out of the deepest sleep she'd ever experienced. She was disoriented when her blurry eyes snapped open.

"You're awake," Cerberus chirped as he picked up the large book Charlotte had a suspicion might have been dropped on purpose. "Cap'in said to wait until you wake and to take you to Cook."

Charlotte blinked, pushing the rest of the sleep away. "Where is Ja—Captain Hades?" She'd barely stopped herself from saying Jack's name, and from the odd look Cerberus had given her, he'd noticed the almost slip.

"He's manning the ship," he answered slowly as if she were simple and he wanted her to understand his words.

Maybe he hadn't noticed her slip of almost saying Jack's name and just thought she wasn't in charge of all her mental faculties.

"Yes, that makes sense. If you'd be so kind as to give me a moment to prepare myself, I will meet you outside the door."

Cerberus continued to stare at her before he nodded and moved toward the door. "Make sure you dress like me." He pointed to his trousers and shirt. He opened the door, but before he closed it, he glanced around both ways and whispered, "Make sure you put your hair up and stuff it under a hat. And you'll be known as Charlie around the men, Cap'in's orders." With the last of his message delivered, he clicked the door closed.

"Cap'in's orders," Charlotte muttered as she cleaned herself up and pinned her hair under the hat she'd been provided. The insufferable man left her asleep and sent his errand boy down to get her. He was ordering her around through a young boy to bring her to the galley so she could act like a woman and cook. He was scared and too cowardly to do it himself. The next time she saw him, she'd push that letter opener farther into his blackened heart.

She inspected herself in the gilded mirror hanging above the desk before leaving the room. Cerberus checked her before nodding in approval.

Charlotte followed him up the narrow stairs to the fresh sea air. The air whipped around her, and she made sure her hat stayed on her head as the wind wanted to reveal who she was, seconds from being out in the open.

They went to a clean room on the top deck that wafted the scent of fresh bread. Charlotte's stomach grumbled as the smell assaulted her nose. At least she'd be in the best room if she had to pretend to be a man. Even if she still had to do a woman's job.

"Cook, this is Charley. He's the new cabin boy." Cerberus introduced her as he went over to the small table in the corner and stuffed a piece of bread in his mouth.

A behemoth of a man turned toward Charlotte, a large knife in one hand. His arms were bare, the shirt sleeves barely covering his huge shoulders, which were covered in colorful tattoos. "Cabin boy? I didn't realize the Cap'in needed a new cabin boy. Are you getting promoted, young Cerb?"

Charlotte surveyed the room as the two talked. Agatha would have drooled at the dried herbs strung around the tidy room. Charlotte was pleasantly surprised at the medicinal herbs she spotted with just one glance. She nodded as she recited the herbs and their uses, pushing her worry away with the exercise. She was secure in the knowledge that when Cook realized she had the cooking capability of a toad, she may be able to convince him to allow her to be the medic for the ship.

Cerberus stood up straight, the bread in his hand forgotten. “No, Cook. The Cap’in rescued Charlie from a bad situation and Cap’in is going to train him before setting him off.”

Charlotte’s eyes widened at the reasoning for her being there. She was surprised Jack had even discussed this strategy with Cerberus in the first place.

“Sorry, lad. You’re in good hands with Cap’in Hades. Now get over there and eat your fill before Cerb stuffs it all in his gullet.”

Charlotte moved over to the small table and pushed a piece of bread in the thick stew she’d been served. She was shocked at how good the food was; she hadn’t been expecting the savory food. She finished off her stew, sopping up the rest of the thick broth with the remainder of her bread.

The cook clapped her hard on the back and she thought he’d dislodged her lung. Cerberus grinned at her, and she noticed he was biting the inside of his cheek to stop himself from laughing.

Charlotte shot him what she hoped was a terrifying look before gathering up the dishes on the table. She walked over to a barrel of water and began scrubbing out the dirty dishes.

"What are you doing?" Cerberus asked in horror.

"Cleaning up the dishes," she replied, confused that she'd put another horrified look on his face.

"We're going to be late, and Cap'in doesn't like it when I'm late." Cerberus shuffled his feet toward the door as if he were going to leave her.

"Late for what?"

Cook took the dishes from her hand and patted her on the back, hard. "Get going with Cerb, lad, I've got this."

Charlotte followed Cerberus out toward the front of the ship where she noticed Jack standing with his legs braced against the wind.

Charlotte stared, attempting to merge the two men in her mind. Jack her savior, and Hades her unknown. His whiskey-colored eyes locked on hers as if he could hear her mind whirling.

"Young Charlie, are you ready for your first day of pirate training?" His booming voice carried past the wind. Charlotte assumed even a cyclone wouldn't be able to drown out Hades if he wanted to be heard.

Cerberus bounced on the balls of his feet, excitement pulsing off him in waves. "I am, Cap'in," he declared, running the rest of the way toward Hades.

"Aye," Charlotte teased, using the affirmative word she'd heard the sailors use as she was carted on the ship.

Hades shot her a winning grin that had her knees melting in an uncomfortable manner. Charlotte mentally slapped herself, refusing to fall at his feet. No, new Charlotte was stronger than that. She would take what he taught her as she did ten years ago when Jack taught her everything he could before he abandoned her. The way she learned what Agatha had taught her.

She would store it all for her future.

Charlotte stalled as she realized she was stronger than even she gave herself credit for. She absorbed and obtained all the information she could possibly find. With the help of Jack, she was able to undo a knot most sailors wouldn't be able to untie. She could sew up, heal, and deliver a baby, if necessary, with the help of Agatha's knowledge.

How did she doubt herself when faced with marrying Lord Sterling? She had many qualifications, and she was going to receive even more training. Charlotte's shoulders went down and back, seeing a future she would be able to dictate right in front of her face. All she had to do was survive being with Hades as he delivered his cargo.

This was possible.

Chapter Nine

"Young Cerberus, where did we leave off?" Hades asked the jumping child, and Charlotte had to force her smile back, not wanting emotions to surface no matter how endearing the two were.

"You were teaching me how to use a sword, Cap'in."

Hades' sharp black eyebrows rose at the young boy's declaration. "I must be slipping in my old age as I remember we were using daggers last time. Charlie, are you ready to be promoted from a letter opener to a dagger?"

Charlotte opened her mouth to say something scathing about how well her letter opener worked last night but held her tongue. Hades was allowing her above deck and teaching her more abilities that would keep her safe. She didn't want to ruin it with her shrewd mouth, especially not in front of his crew. Even though he hadn't said it to her before he abandoned her yet again, she had an inkling he wouldn't appreciate her giving him a scathing remark in front of his men.

He watched her as she nodded instead of letting her words fly. He inclined his head with a slight motion, something she wasn't even positive she'd have noticed if she hadn't been watching for it.

"Go get the boards, Cerberus."

"But Cap'in," the boy whined as he moved over to a basket Charlotte hadn't noticed before.

"You know the rules, Master Cerb. Would you like to explain them to Master Charlie?"

Cerberus brought over the basket and two small stools, putting them next to a larger stool. Cerberus' lip jutted out in a pout and Charlotte was even more intrigued.

"We have to do our letters and numbers before Cap'in will let us do the fun stuff." The dejected look on the boy's face made Charlotte smile. "I just thought since we have Charlie here, we would be able to skip this part today. You know, for Charlie." The hopeful expression on his face solidified Charlotte's smile.

"Why would I do that?" Hades asked. His voice was stern, but Charlotte noticed the corner of his beard twitched.

The boy opened his mouth to answer but snapped it shut, realizing the trap he was almost maneuvered in. Thoroughly thwarted, Cerb handed Charlotte a small board and a piece of chalk.

"It ain't fair, Cap'in," Cerb cried as Charlotte moved around Hades, learning how to handle the intricate dagger he'd handed her.

Charlotte, already knowing her numbers and letters, finished her lesson quickly, leaving Cerberus to pout and give Charlotte mean pirate glares.

"How is that?" Hades asked, deftly evading Charlotte as she lunged forward with her dagger. "Charlie finished his lessons and now he gets to move on to his other lessons. As soon as you've mastered your letters and numbers lesson for today, you will also be allowed to move on to daggers."

"But—" Cerberus stopped when Hades glared at him with a look that had Charlotte take a step back.

"Lessons are done for today. Go ask Cook if he needs help for dinner tonight."

Charlotte expected Cerb to argue, but he nodded, placing his chalk and board back in the basket. His shoulders were hunched as he moved to leave the area. Before he walked down the stairs, he squared his shoulders and turned. "I wasn't going to say anything, Cap'in. I can be trusted. I apologize."

"Thank you for the apology. I know you can be trusted, but we can't have any slips. It's of the utmost importance that we ensure Charlie is safe here. I'll see you tomorrow." Hades acknowledged his apology but didn't rescind his punishment.

When the boy was out of earshot, Charlotte whirled on him. "Why didn't you let him practice? He apologized."

"He could have ruined everything by giving away who you are. I'm not putting your life in peril because a young pup wants to play with daggers. This is true pirate training. If he wants to man his own ship when he's older, he needs to know everything I'm teaching him even the lessons on how to keep one's mouth shut."

Charlotte threw out her arms and turned a full circle. "There isn't anyone near us to overhear."

He took a menacing step toward her and Charlotte held her ground as much as she wanted to back up. "I'm not putting your life in danger on chance."

Charlotte's heartbeat sped up as he neared. His large presence and his declaration did funny things to her stomach, and she hated it.

"Hades," a man shouted, breaking them out of their trance.

"It seems you need to follow your own rules, Hades." Charlotte flicked the dagger between them.

"You are correct," he conceded before turning toward the rough-looking sailor coming their way. "Keep to me and don't say a word," he whispered before the sailor was close enough to hear.

"What is it, Shark?"

Charlotte attempted to study the man as he came near, but before she could get a look at the burly pirate, Hades stepped in front of her.

Charlotte wondered if everyone on this ship was large in one way or another.

"We were wondering if you were going to finish with the young pup soon and meet with us on what the plans are?" His tone was anything but respectful and Hades' back went stiff at the contempt in Shark's voice.

"I didn't know you were the spokesperson for my ship, Shark. I will debrief *my* crew when I feel the need to do so. If you want your portion of the payout, I will remind you only once to never question me. Do you understand me?"

Charlotte shivered at the coldness in Hades' question. She was certain if Shark answered incorrectly, he would be gutted right there on the deck.

"Yes, Hades. We wanted to ensure this journey went right, as this is the largest cargo we've ever had."

"Captain," was the only answer Hades gave him. He didn't answer the implied question. He stated his name and waited, the dagger in his hand held in a lethal grip.

"Yes, Captain," Shark answered with all the respect you would think a captain of a pirate ship would receive.

Charlotte wasn't fooled by Shark's capitulation, and by the continued grip of the dagger, she knew Hades wasn't as well.

"Your lessons are over today, Charlie," Hades said, still not removing his deadly stare from Shark's retreating back. "I'll take you back to the quarters. I want you to polish and dust the room before supper tonight."

Charlotte followed Hades to the room, sending covert glances to the crew, wanting to get a read on them. They were a motley bunch and none of them matched. Some of the men were fat while others were skin and bones. And while some were dressed in rags, others wore impeccable clothing.

Some openly sneered at her while others gawked at her with curiosity.

"Who's the new pup, Cap'in?" one of the jollier-looking men asked.

All activity stopped as they waited for Hades' reply. "This is Charley. I rescued him when we docked. He's a little shy, but with the right training, he'll be a better pirate than any of you lot."

Most of the men laughed jovially. "We'll get him some real pirate training when we dock in the colonies. Young Charlie, I'll pay for your first docking when we get to port. Ida will teach you right."

Charlotte's ears burned under the hat still firmly over her hair, as she understood their meaning.

Hades laughed and clapped her on the back, almost having her sprawled out in front of his men. "We'll make him a real pirate yet."

The men were still laughing and comparing different women Charlie should be broken in with as they went down the stairs to the captain's quarters.

When the heavy wood door closed out the noise of the ship, Charlotte pinned him with her glare. "They were talking about..." she sputtered to a stop, not knowing the correct word.

"Port doxies. Whores. Yes, Pet." He ushered her toward the desk, and she noticed another chair flanking the desk that wasn't there before.

"If they are the professionals your crew makes them out to be, I'm fairly sure they'll recognize I'm not a cabin boy rather quickly."

A sputtering sound had Charlotte's attention moving from the new chair to Hades staring at her in disbelief.

"Pardon."

"Pardon denied," Charlotte shot back just how he had said to her the day he kidnapped her. "I don't know why you'd even request a pardon, Hades. You of all people know I don't have the undercarriage of a man and I'm certain even a non-professional doxy would figure that out."

She wasn't certain, but she thought maybe he was blushing. She didn't move her gaze from him, letting it penetrate into his soul. He told her she'd be free as soon as they unloaded the cargo in the colonies, but he didn't think about how she'd get to that point. How she was going to survive on a ship full of degenerate pirates.

"What are you planning, Hades?" She couldn't stop saying his pirate's name, wanting to remind herself he wasn't her Jack anymore. "You're going to keep me stuck in here and doing pirate lessons with Cerberus. Your crew is going to get suspicious."

He rubbed his hand over his face, scratching his beard. "I am aware of all of this, Pet. I was planning to slowly introduce you as Charlie to the crew. Yes, you are going to have to hear some language and stories a lady shouldn't ever have to hear.

They are going to tease you, but unless I can think of another story, you're going to have to endure it. I had Cerberus and Jackal start a rumor as to why you're aboard."

Charlotte had the urge to go and comfort him, but she remained strong where she was standing. He still kidnapped her and brought her aboard a pirate ship. Even though she understood his intentions, she didn't want to be so weak she fell into his arms immediately.

"And what rumor would that be? Remember, Hades, we aren't keeping anything from each other. Full disclosure."

"I rescued you from a man who kept you captive and mistreated you. I saw him whipping you in the street and stopped him."

"Whipping me?"

"Yes, it will explain why you keep your shirt on all the time. Also, you were so scared you don't want to be around the crew, which is why you are sleeping in my quarters on a cot I had brought in."

Charlotte had been so enthralled by the new chair she hadn't noticed the cot stuffed in the corner of the room.

"I need you to be Charlie when you're above deck and I need you to stay with Cerberus at all times. He and Jackal are the only ones aboard who know about your true identity. And I need you to stay far away from Shark."

He stepped closer, invading her space. Charlotte's neck fell back so she could see into his eyes. His large, calloused hand wrapped around the bottom of her chin, keeping her gaze locked on him. "Promise me, Pet. Promise me you'll stay with Cerberus and keep your distance from Shark. If you do that, we will pull this off and you'll be living in a life of luxury when we get back."

His finger stroked the side of her cheek as he continued to cradle her chin. Charlotte felt faint at the nearness of him. The gentleness he showed her had her wanting to throw herself into his arms.

"I promise." Her declaration was breathy, and she would have been embarrassed if it weren't for the blaze in his whiskey-colored eyes.

"I only want you to be happy. I've only ever wanted you to be happy."

Charlotte wanted to scream at him that if that was true, he wouldn't have left her alone ten years ago. It was unfair, she knew it, and stating it would be childish. He may have seemed like he was older and more worldly than she had been, but he was right to say he was a kid when he killed Mr. Dons. He had done something no child should ever have to do, and to make him feel guilty for his choice to run away was wrong. She had selfishly held onto her anger toward him because she had only wanted him.

Stepping back and looking at it through his eyes, she knew her anger was unwarranted. And the only person who deserved her anger was Mr. Dons, and being that he had been dead for ten years it felt as if even he didn't deserve the energy of her anger any longer.

"You shouldn't care about my happiness. I've cursed you for years. I was angry with you for leaving me. I understand you had to leave now, and it was so unfair how upset I was that you did what you had to do to survive."

"No, Pet, I left you alone. I had convinced myself you would be better off without me. It was easier than to wonder how awful your father and brother were treating you. When you found Agatha, it was even easier to convince myself you were where you belonged even though I was jealous of a haggard, old healer and the time she got to spend with you."

His confession healed more of the residual anger lingering in her wounded soul. "I'm here now."

His fingers flexed on her jaw before he lowered his mouth toward hers. This kiss was different from the first. The frantic claiming of the last one was now replaced with a slow possession.

Heat, delicious and confusing, infused her lower belly. Charlotte attempted to copy what he was doing, learning from him once again. His thumb stroked around her jaw.

"Relax, Lot," he whispered inside of her mouth, letting his tongue stroke her bottom lip.

"I don't know what I'm doing. I was trying to do what you were doing." She wasn't embarrassed admitting this to him. She had never held back with Jack, and she wouldn't start now.

"You were always a fast learner, but I don't want you to copy me, Pet. I want you to feel. Be you. Be Charlotte. You've been stuck for too long not to be anything else."

Charlotte gripped onto his shirt. His words pushed into her, expanding and filling some of the emptiness she had gotten accustomed to for such a long time. She forgot what her life felt like without the clawing loneliness in the pit of her stomach.

Tears rushed up her throat, leaving a path of fire. She swallowed to staunch the flood of emotion. She blinked back the burning traveling behind her eyes.

"I..." she began to speak, but words refused to unjumble in her brain.

He watched her with his whiskey-colored eyes, hiding the emotion behind them. He nodded as if he'd made a decision he'd been pondering. "I'll have a bath sent down. You're going to be sore tomorrow, but you're strong. You'll get through it. I'll get you through this journey and settled somewhere you can explore who Charlotte Fitzwilliam's truly is as a free woman. With no obstacles."

He stepped around her and walked out the door, her mouth agape at his quick departure. Standing still, she placed her fingers to her lips where the taste of him lingered, dark and dangerous, yet somehow comforting. She thought back to all those years ago when her life had been turned upside down and with a self-satisfied smirk, she was certain he didn't kiss Mary the way he'd just kissed her.

The bath was wonderful. She soaked her aching joints in the scalding water. Cerberus wanted to cool it down, but Charlotte wouldn't have it as she knew the heat would leach from the water too soon as it was. No reason to waste any of the soothing warmth.

Chapter Ten

After she dried herself off, she pulled on another pair of trousers and bound her breasts before pulling on a large shirt. She jumped when there was a knock at the door, regretting the move almost immediately as it gave her sore muscles the ability to voice their grievances at their misuse.

"Come in," she called after hastily stuffing her hair up in a woven hat that stretched to accommodate the mass. She was certain none of the crew would make it down to the captain's quarters without permission, but she wasn't going to get caught with her hair down.

Hades strolled in. His heated gaze traveled down the length of her body. Once again, the heat she was becoming accustomed to when Hades' eyes collided with hers, simmered in her belly.

"I see you're dressed." His voice was gravelly and made the simmering turn into a boil. He cleared his throat. "You can let your hair down. We'll be eating in here tonight. Cerberus will be delivering our dinner shortly."

Charlotte frowned even though she was grateful she wouldn't have to dine with a motley crew of pirates. "Won't your crew get suspicious if you keep me locked down here?" Her voice went low and husky when she said locked and from the flare in his eyes, he also heard the change in pitch.

"Yes, you'll have to start dining with them soon. I figured a reprieve for tonight wouldn't cause too many tongues to waggle. You worked hard at training today."

She swallowed her disappointment. The conflicting feelings bombarding her brain already confused her, and more decisions were making her brain feel crowded. She hoped when decisions about her future were finally made, there would be more room for her to think.

The knock on the door broke through her thoughts. Thoughts she wasn't going to be able to untangle at the moment. Hades pulled the door open to young Cerberus carrying a large silver tray covered with a beautiful silver topper.

After Cerberus delivered the food, scuttling away as quickly as he could to get back to the rowdy crew, Charlotte raised an eyebrow at the ornate silver dish.

Jack smiled—no, Hades smiled. The mischievous glint in his eyes was all pirate. "I do enjoy some of the spoils of my profession. I'm not a saint." The wink he sent her had everything in her go molten hot.

He gestured for her to sit down as he pulled the cover off, revealing two heaping bowls of hearty stew. Charlotte's stomach growled as the scents assaulted her nose.

"You need to eat more. The sea makes a person ravenous, and you'll be hungrier as you continue your training."

Charlotte was embarrassed at the betrayal of her stomach, but when the stew was set in front of her, she clutched her spoon with no chance it would get away.

"Eat," Hades commanded. "The closer to the colonies we get, the less decadent the fare gets. Cook does have some of the crew fish when they can to keep us from eating hard biscuits, but even fish gets redundant."

Charlotte took a dainty sip of the stew and her stomach screamed again, making its hunger prevalent. She took another tiny sip, wanting to devour the bowl.

Hades tucked into his food and with a quick glance, Charlotte was relieved he wasn't paying attention to her. With his focus elsewhere, she shoveled the food in her mouth. When she scraped the last of the stew in her mouth, she smiled at the contentment of a full stomach.

"Would you like some more?"

Charlotte jumped, forgetting he was even in front of her as she ravaged her food. She waited a moment before answering, wanting to make sure she answered him truthfully. "I'm full. Thank you."

He nodded, loading up the plates back on the tray, then set the covered tray outside for who she assumed was Cerberus to pick up.

Charlotte snatched the hat off her head and pulled her fingers through the knotted mess. Hades watched her. His back leaned against the door as he tracked the movement of her fingers. With a deep, fortifying breath, he approached her.

"Would you allow me?" He pulled out an ivory-handled brush from his trunk.

Charlotte's stomach flipped at the sultry question. The room felt as if it shrank from his nearness. Their gazes were locked on each other. All noises, all life vanished as they continued to stay connected.

"Yes." It was her turn to clear her throat. The words *take me, make me yours, be mine* played over her tongue. *Stay with me, never let me go* clogged her windpipe.

He nodded, and Charlotte wondered if the words pushed hard enough on the back of her mouth that he could read the silent plea. He stretched out his hand. As if in a trance, Charlotte placed hers in his. His fingers engulfed her hand. His large and sun-kissed skin, while hers were pale and small.

He led her to the bed, where he sat her down and climbed behind her. Charlotte was aware of every brush of his body against hers. She stared at a knot in the wood as she listened to him settle himself on a pillow as he leaned against the wall. His strong arms wrapped around her waist and dragged her between his stretched-out legs.

Charlotte sucked in a deep breath as his heat seared into her back. She ordered herself not to lean against him like she wanted to. His hand followed the brush as he started from the tip of her long locks, languidly making his way through her hair.

Charlotte's heart pounded in her ears, and she focused on the knot in the wood as she melted in his touch. Her eyes grew blurry, and the knot lost all semblance of keeping her grounded in the moment. Her eyelids grew heavy. The strenuous training fatigued her muscles into submission just as Hades was bringing her thick locks into line.

With a jerk, Charlotte caught herself leaning fully into Hades' strong chest. His hands wrapped around her shoulders, guiding her back to him. She wanted to protest, knowing her leaning on him as the hard wood pressed against his back wasn't comfortable, but her lips wouldn't work.

A knock on the door brought her back to life for the second day in a row. Without opening her eyes, she knew Hades wasn't in the room with her. She moved and bit her lip at her protesting muscles. She had expected to be sore from the physical training she'd endured, but she hadn't expected them to hate her. She remembered her muscles hurting when she practiced with Jack all those years ago, yet they never were as sore as they were at that moment.

"Come in, Cerb," she called, knowing she wasn't making it to the door anytime soon.

Cerb strode in with a large smile on his face. His face paled when he noticed her struggling to move around the room. "Are you sick?" he asked, his large eyes filled with concern.

Charlotte shot him a reassuring smile as she began pulling the hat on her head. She stopped when she realized her hair had been neatly plaited, making it easy to coil on top of her head before pulling the hat on.

Her cheeks burned when she remembered Hades pulling the brush through her hair and falling into one of the safest slumbers she'd had in a long time.

"I'm sore from yesterday's training," she admitted as she checked herself in the mirror to make sure she was more Charlie than Charlotte.

“You’re not too sore to train today, are you? Cap’in said we’d be learning together, and I don’t know what he’d do if you couldn’t train.” Cerberus was rubbing his hands together in worry.

Charlotte smiled more, realizing he wasn’t worried about her, but he was worried she would ruin his chance of touching a dagger again. Her heart swelled, knowing even on a pirate ship, he still retained some of his childlike innocence.

“No, I’m perfectly capable of getting through training today. In fact, I was going to ask if you’d like me to assist you with your letters and numbers during dinner?”

Cerberus scrunched up his face at the offer. Charlotte hurried to fix her error. “Captain Hades informed me I would be dining with the crew on deck soon and I don’t want to give myself away with a silly mistake. If you would keep me occupied by letting me teach you your letters and numbers, it will surely keep me from making a blunder. Also, you seem like an intelligent young man. I have a feeling you’ll have your letters and numbers mastered before we get to the colonies, giving you more time to practice with weapons.”

That had done it. Cerberus’ scrunched face lit up with delight as he listened to her bargain. He may dislike the thought of extra studying, but to get to practice with weapons faster was an easy decision for the young pirate.

"I would be happy to keep you occupied during dinner. As long as it doesn't take longer than eating. The crew is teaching me how to play the flute, and a proper pirate should also know how to play the flute." His face was sincere, and Charlotte resisted the urge to pull him into a fierce hug.

Charlotte nodded in agreement. She saw how badly Cerberus wanted to be accepted by the men on deck and she wouldn't stifle him with her loneliness. As much as she wanted to keep her new friend to herself, she knew he would resist if she attempted to steal more time from him away from the men on deck.

After finishing her morning ablutions, Charlotte followed Cerberus to Cook, hiding her cringes from her aching muscles with every step. Charlotte had to stop the groan from escaping her tortured lips when she lifted her legs to climb the steep steps to the deck. She ate the sweetened oatmeal Cook sat in front of her slowly. Cerb finished his food quickly, tapping his foot on the floor as he watched every excruciatingly slow bite Charlotte took. He exhaled deeply when she finished her bowl.

Charlotte smiled as she handed Cook her plate before letting Cerb lead her out into the blinding light.

Before she was dragged toward another harsh training session, Charlotte asked Cook for a bit of willow tree bark. Cook smiled widely, showing off a missing front tooth and the one next to it encased in gold as he handed her the bark. After swallowing the willow bark, she allowed Cerb to lead her outside, hoping the effects of the pain reliever would kick in quickly. Charlotte winced at the brightness. With no trees or buildings to block the sun, it was splayed across the deck as she allowed Cerb to lead her toward Hades.

Jackal smacked her on the back. "You'll get used to it, Charlie."

As she continued to follow Cerb blindly, she barely stopped herself from toppling over.

Charlotte was surprised when she realized she wasn't sad Jackal no longer called her little bird. She recognized she wasn't that girl anymore. *Heck, I'm on my second day of pirate training,* she thought proudly. And having a second day meant she made it through her first day. Charlotte was a survivor. She wasn't a lost little bird anymore. She was learning to fly and once again it was because of Jack.

Charlotte slowed her work down, intending to finish when Cerb finished so he wouldn't get antsy watching her engage in dagger training.

"Charlie, are you having an issue?" Hades asked close to her ear. She jumped, not aware he had snuck up on her.

She shook her head and clenched the chalk until it snapped.

"I think you're stalling."

"I was taking my time so I could practice with Cerb," she admitted.

"Get up," he ordered, still close to her ear. The harsh tone had gooseflesh running up her arm.

Cerb's head shot up and the pure want in his face broke her heart. Hades stepped in front of him, blocking her view.

"You're almost finished, Cerb. Concentrate and finish your task. A pirate understands their priorities."

Cerb nodded and went back to his board with vigor. Charlotte wanted to argue with Hades. She wanted to tell him he was being too hard on the young pirate, but she kept her mouth shut, not knowing where Shark was on the ship. Charlotte followed Hades to the makeshift area where they practiced daggers the day before and vowed to herself to help Cerb learn as quickly as he could so he wouldn't be left behind.

"Are you sore today?" he asked as he handed her the ornate, jeweled dagger she'd used the day before.

"I'm feeling better. I took willow bark from Cook this morning and it feels as if it is working," she admitted, not feeling ashamed at the admission. Yes, she was strong, but she also knew when to tell the truth.

"Good." Hades nodded, not making eye contact with her as they both stared at the blade in her hand.

"This is beautiful." She was amazed at how well balanced it was in her hand as if it was made for her.

"Shall we start?"

Charlotte wanted to see his face, but the blinding sun made it impossible when she glanced up to see him. She squinted her eyes, making them water from the brightness.

"I can't see," she whispered as if the omission would make her weak.

"Use your other senses. Close your eyes."

"Close my eyes?" she snapped.

"Yes, there will be times it will be too dark or too light. You'll need to learn how to trust your instincts. Now close your eyes or I'll blindfold you."

Charlotte glared at him and hoped he could see it before she closed her eyes. Her senses assailed her. The roar of the ocean slapping the side of the ship. The raucous laughter of the crew. The flapping of the sails as the wind pushed them to their destination.

She inhaled the salty scent of the water, allowing it to fill her lungs. The next inhale had a subtle change; the dark hints of Hades invaded her nostrils. She knew he was getting close.

She gripped the dagger as she pushed the sound of the water away, listening intently for his steps. She heard the wood give to her left, but she didn't react, not wanting him to know she was aware of his movements. His scent became stronger with another creek of the wood. Charlotte's hand twitched, but she refused to move, wanting him to get closer. Sweat coated her palm, but she held on to the dagger.

She felt the shift of energy, which had nothing to do with the wind. She pulled up her dagger and stopped when she felt resistance.

"Good." His mouth was at her ear.

Charlotte opened her eyes to see her dagger pointed at his chest. They were both breathing deeply, his scent making her lightheaded. The sun still blotted out most of his face, but if it was anything like hers, the blatant want was plastered all over.

"Done," Cerberus called, breaking the spell between them.

They pulled apart quickly. "Very good. Are you ready to learn without your eyes?" Hades sounded like the pirate master he was, but Charlotte heard the annoyance in his voice for being interrupted.

"Without my eyes?" Cerb asked with adorable innocence.

For hours, Cerb and Charlotte practiced protecting themselves from their assailants without their sight. And for those hours, Charlotte was fully aware of Hades. His smell, his breathing, his being had invaded her senses.

"That will be all for today," Hades stated.

Sweat drenched the blindfold he put on her when Cerb had joined them.

She breathed deeply, pulling the blindfold off her face and mopping the sweat with the damp cloth. Cerb was grinning next to her, his face red with exertion. Charlotte closed her eyes, hoping she didn't look as disgusting as Cerb did.

"Go get cleaned up the both of you and I'll meet you up here for dinner in two hours." Hades dismissed them.

Charlotte ran down the stairs, wanting to get away from him before he saw how disheveled she looked.

"No bath today, young Charlie."

Charlotte wanted to shoot him a glare, but she was aware the crew was in hearing distance and having a young cabin boy in training mock the captain would be a stupid move. She knew he was teasing her, and she bit the sides of her lips to keep from smiling.

Chapter Eleven

Charlotte ripped off the hat as soon as the door closed. Her hair was sweaty as she undid the braid, allowing it to dry in the air. She poured the tepid water in the basin and began her ablutions. She moaned as the water wiped away the grime of the sweat she'd accumulated.

Her muscles protested, but she felt accomplished. She didn't give up. She swung her dagger with as much, if not more, accuracy than Cerb. She felt strong as if she could achieve any goal she had. Now she just needed to decide what her goal was.

Charlotte refused to wipe her sweaty palms on her trousers when she walked into the dining room. The room was loud and smelled of unwashed men. Charlotte stilled her face. She would not show them any weakness. She just hoped Cook made something to overpower the stench coming from the crew.

Cerb led her to a quiet corner where he'd already set up the boards and pieces of chalk. He glanced longingly over at the rowdy pirates shoveling food in their gaping mouths, talking around the bites they were chewing.

“I won’t take long to eat,” she promised him, schooling her features when she scanned the room for Hades. She was disappointed when she didn’t see his face in the crowd.

Cook set down two plates with chicken and rice piled high. Charlotte tucked into her food, not worrying about manners as she was supposed to be a pirate in training. If she was too delicate, the crew would notice.

Charlotte and Cerb went over his letters, and he caught on quickly when she found out he learned more by listening than seeing.

“Whatcha two horses trotters doing?” Shark asked, stumbling over toward them with a jug of rum hanging off his index finger.

“Nothing that concerns you,” Cerb quipped, his eyes trained on the drunken man.

“Oh, this ship is my concern. Hades is getting soft, letting scraggly vermin on the ship. I need to make sure this ship stays headed in the right direction.”

“Maybe you should discuss your concerns with Hades,” Charlotte shot back, instantly wishing she’d kept her mouth shut.

Shark grinned at her with a mouth full of missing teeth or blackened ones barely hanging on, which made Charlotte almost cast up her accounts. “Maybe I should slit your throat.” He leaned against the table, his filthy hands on the clean wood.

“Maybe you should go finish your bottle somewhere else.” She once again couldn’t seem to keep her mouth shut.

Shark moved, but in his inebriated state, Charlotte was faster. She put her dagger in between his fingers, barely missing the thin skin in between the digits. Shark glanced down to where she still held on to the dagger.

Jackal came over, standing behind Charlotte and Cerb. The rowdy room was now quiet. “Are you causing my boy problems?” Jackal asked, his hand on Cerb’s shoulder.

“I was just making sure the pups didn’t need anything,” Shark answered, his hand stealthily moving away from the dagger.

Charlotte wanted to scoff. Shark reminded her of her brother, Alexander. They were strong when there wasn’t anyone bigger than them around. It was funny how she could find similarities between her brother, who was a member of the ton, and a swarthy pirate. Both of them left a bad taste in her mouth.

“Are you two done?” Jackal asked, not taking his hand off Cerb.

"We are." Charlotte stood up, grabbed Cerb's empty plate and walked it over to the wash bucket.

"Cerb, take Charlie down to the captain's room. He hasn't fully recovered from his ordeal on land."

Charlotte and Cerb walked slowly out of the dining room, not wanting the crew to think they were running away from the coward.

Charlotte thanked Cerb at the door before walking into the room and closing the thick hunk of wood and pushing Shark out of her thoughts.

She gasped when she turned to see Hades standing in the tub. His hands scrubbed vigorously at his hair. She studied—no, memorized his muscular body. She devoured the sun-touched skin, which stopped at his waist. His stomach was taut, with lines dividing it lengthwise and widthwise. A smattering of dark hair cleaved between his pectoral muscles and when she followed the grooves to the forbidden sight, her whole body ignited.

Charlotte stared, her mouth hanging open as she took in the entirety of his length. She hadn't been paying attention the night he took her virginity and realized she hadn't noticed his lower area. She was too much in shock and too much in her own scheme to fully take in the sight in front of her, but she was fully aware at that moment.

As she stared at his length, she was startled to see it extended farther, the heavy member pointing straight at her.

"Lot, you're killing me," Jack groaned.

He covered his member with the towel, breaking her trance. She met his eyes, prepared for the mocking she was certain she'd see, but instead, fire burned in them. The simmering whenever he was near warmed her lower belly and moved through her limbs until she felt drugged from the liquid heat coursing through her.

"How was dinner?" He didn't know it, but his question was one of the few that could be asked to douse the fire running through her veins.

"It was almost uneventful." She wanted to lie to him but knew if she didn't tell him what happened, Cerb, Jackal, or anyone else would relay the events to him.

"Cerb and I had a small run-in with Shark," she started hesitantly.

His eyes sharpened, locking in on hers. "How small? And remember we promised no lies between us."

She sighed her dread because she knew he was right. If she asked for full disclosure, she would have to reciprocate in kind.

She told him the details of dinner, not keeping anything from him but keeping her voice calm so as not to upset him further.

When she was done with the short tale, he was heading toward the door.

"Stop," she commanded.

His hand stayed on the doorknob. He didn't turn it to depart nor did he turn his body.

"He was just bullying us as most pirates are going to do with new recruits. I stood my ground."

"Yes, and now you're a target." He seethed.

"I've always been a target. Now he knows I will fight back. If you go out there, he'll know I told you and I'll be even more of a target."

"And I'm supposed to allow him to disparage the way I run this ship?"

She thought of this as well, knowing he would argue this point. "No, but the other crew members didn't back him. He's alone in his thinking and he knows it. Jackal stopped the escalation, and he'll tell you about it tomorrow when you can handle it. Now I need my hair brushed."

She held her breath, watching his knuckles go white on the doorknob as he made his decision on whether to listen to her or to retaliate. He finally let go of the tarnished knob and she let the breath she was holding whoosh out of her.

Without a word, she retrieved the brush as Hades settled on the bed in the same position they were the night before. With the same gentleness as the other night, he ran the brush through her hair. Charlotte relaxed into his touch immediately, once again falling asleep to the rhythm of his breathing and the brush strokes.

***

Two weeks had gone by, the ocean now the constant background to Charlotte's life.

With a mischievous smile, Charlotte threw open the door before Cerb could knock. "I didn't think you were ever going to get here." She shot him a cheeky wink before walking ahead of him for the first time since Cerb had knocked on her door.

Charlotte's body and mind slowly became accustomed to the rigorous training. She would have beat Cerb to the door the day before, but she got carried away with the muscle definition she was gaining in her arms.

Charlotte couldn't shake the pride she'd felt at seeing actual changes in her body. Her arms were stronger, as well as her legs, and when she was washing last night, she noticed her stomach was flatter, with some lines of her own.

Charlotte hurried to eat, scarfing down her breakfast as soon as Cook set it in front of her. She braced herself when his meaty hand clapped her on the back and smiled widely when it didn't send her flying.

This time it was her tapping her foot, waiting for Cerb to finish his food so they could begin that day's pirate training. She had fallen into a comfortable pattern, Shark was the only one who ruined it with his nightly bullying. He didn't go as far as he went the first night she'd put her dagger in between his fingers, and she felt that was a victory for her. Charlotte didn't hide her self-satisfied grin. Every time he'd come over to terrorize her and Cerb, he'd clench his hands into fists the moment she touched her dagger.

The bullying was tolerable, especially as more and more of the crew seemed to get fed up with Shark's constant banter and yelled at him more quickly to leave the cabin boys alone.

After finishing his food, Cerb and Charlotte made their way to the deck where Hades was waiting for them. She noticed something was off the moment she made it up the short set of steps to get to him. The usual smirk he wore was replaced with a crease as he watched whatever had captured his attention behind her.

"Hello, lads." His words were chipper, but the worry threaded in them had Charlotte on alert.

"Training is going to be different today," he explained, still watching the distance behind her.

Charlotte's heart lurched. She wouldn't admit it to Hades, only to herself, that her favorite part of the day was when she finished her lessons well beyond Cerb, and she and Hades had a moment alone to practice together. Well, that wasn't true. Her favorite part of her day was after her dinner, when she'd climb between Hades' legs as he brushed her hair.

The sly brushes of his hands against her were a thrill she lived for. Heat would rush through her body the moment she was done with her lessons and walking toward Hades. His confident, knowing smile always firmly in place.

She wondered if he'd finally got fed up with Cerb finishing his lessons more quickly because of her nightly tutelage. He grumbled the last few nights about not having enough time with her because Cerb interrupted at the most inopportune time.

Charlotte was well aware she wouldn't hold off her affection for Hades much longer. His strenuous training during the day and his gentle treatment of her at night had her falling in love with the man he was now and no longer the figment of her childhood fascination. She was certain Hades was also aware of this fact as his touches at night were becoming bolder.

His words against her ear as he relayed what he'd done for the day now ended with a kiss to her lobe. When she would fall asleep, she'd feel his arms wrap around her. He'd only relinquish his hold on her body in the morning, yet his arms lingered longer with every waking morning.

Her morning routine now involved watching him ready himself through slitted lids, not wanting him to know how utterly entranced she was by his being. He would in turn watch her before tucking the loose hair that escaped her plait during the night. Brushing the softest of kisses over her cheek before clearing his throat, most likely regaining his Hades persona and walking out the door.

Charlotte and Cerb reached him, not knowing what was in store for them with the fierceness mapping over his face.

"Turn around, lads, and tell me what you see," he ordered them.

He stepped behind her as she noticed the ominous clouds blanketing the sky, blotting out everything behind them.

"Those clouds appear to be heading our way," Charlotte answered, pushing down her fear. She had read numerous stories about the weather taking its revenge on the ocean and anything gracing the salt-encrusted water, including the ship she was currently on. Tossing ships as if they were toys stuck in a toddler's tantrum.

"Very good, Charlie." He handed her a spyglass and Charlotte pressed it to her eye, noticing just how angry the storm appeared.

She dutifully handed the spyglass to Cerberus, hoping neither of them noted her shaking hands. When they both had their fill of the roiling clouds, Hades retrieved the spyglass.

"I need both of you to be good lads and go down on deck. Be smart, use your heads, and help wherever you are needed. Do not get in the way as we batten down the ship. As soon as the wind begins to whip around, I need both of you in your rooms, and I want you to stay there. We will get through this storm and at times you'll feel as if we are going to sink. I won't let that happen."

Charlotte swallowed and glanced at Cerb, who looked better off than she felt.

"Trust me," he ordered. Although it was said to both of them, Charlotte felt as if the words were more for her and not just about the impending storm.

"Yes, Captain," they both agreed in unison.

"Good, now go."

Charlotte watched his hand in the periphery of her vision rise as if to touch her, but he stopped abruptly, catching himself before he could make contact. Even though he hadn't touched her, Charlotte felt his presence at her back. She felt his need, his undeniable want, and she had to bite her tongue so as not to tell him she felt the same.

"Be safe," he whispered before clapping them both on the shoulders, dismissing them to their mission.

Charlotte wanted to tell him to be safe as well, but she knew her place and at the moment, she was Charlie, the apprentice to the pirate captain and not Charlotte, the woman falling in love with the captain.

Cerb went directly to Jackal as they coiled rope thicker than Charlotte's thigh. Charlotte noticed Shark lurking around. Not wanting to deal with him as well as her terror for the impending storm, she went the other way, avoiding him altogether. She moved at a fast pace toward Cook, hoping she could be of some use to the man she was slowly thinking of as a friend.

"Young Charlie, come to help me?"

"Yes." The waver in her voice frustrated her. She pushed her fear aside and tried again. "Captain wanted us to help where we could before we have to go to our rooms to wait out the storm. I'm not supposed to get in the way, and I decided to check with you first."

"Good, man." He clapped her on the back. Oddly enough, the hard pat settled her nerves.

They worked quietly, letting Charlotte know Cook might not have been as settled as he pretended. Charlotte helped Cook get food ready as the crew was going to be up all night, battling the elements. She locked down what she could, but Cook wasn't a novice and his kitchen was mostly ready for what was to come.

Wind whistled as the storm barreled down on the ship. "Get to your quarters, young Charlie. Don't light a lamp. It is going to get rocky, and we don't want to have to deal with a fire as well as Mother Nature." Cook handed her a cloth filled with food and rushed her out of the kitchen.

"Should I bring some to Cerb?" she asked before she was fully pushed out.

"He'll come before he goes. You get down and get ready for a ride."

Charlotte held on to her food and her hat as she made her way to the captain's quarters. She attempted to find Hades, but the wind and the mayhem on deck made it impossible. A gust tried to rip her hat and her food away, making her move even faster.

The crew reminded her of an ant hill when water was splashed on it. They were running around in organized chaos. She thought she caught a glimpse of Hades, but she couldn't turn fast enough to find him. Darkness descended on the ship as a fat raindrop landed on Charlotte's nose, right before she hit the stairs.

Chapter Twelve

Charlotte braced herself as the ship rolled. She attempted to lie on the bed, but as soon as the storm sank its claws into the ship, she realized how silly that thought was. She wedged the chair under the desk after she'd picked it up for the third time. The first time it fell, the crash had an unexpected scream rip from her throat, showing her nerves to the empty room.

The ship rose and she knew now what she was about to experience. She wedged herself in between the bed and the wall, holding her breath as the ship dropped. Her fingers gripped the walls for purchase. She sucked in a breath as she free-fell. The ship lurched as it plummeted, slapping the water with a hard thwack right before it rose again to repeat the process.

Charlotte's fingers ached from holding on. Her muscles screamed as they were locked with fear and nausea. Her head ached from grinding her back teeth. The ship leaned precariously to the side, and tears threatened to leak out.

"Why can't it pick a direction?" she questioned as the ship went up and down, then to the left and right.

She trusted Hades to keep the ship from breaking apart and sinking to the bottom of the ocean, but as the ship continued to creak and roll, doubts floated through her mind.

"He promised we wouldn't sink," she muttered repeatedly as tears continued to run down her cheeks.

A loud, horrible crack sounded over the din of the storm. Screams from above overrode the winds hold on the night's noise. The sound of terrified men were now the only thing she could hear and she wished for the sound of the wind to come back. Charlotte's stomach pitched as she listened to screams and shouting above deck.

Charlotte cried as she continued to listen to the clamor above her. Her whole body hurt from holding on and she begged it would be over soon.

A loud knock landed on the door. It took Charlotte a minute to realize it wasn't the ship breaking apart and the ocean calling her to their dark, inky depths. Another knock hit the wooden door.

Charlotte wrenched her body away from the wall. She ricocheted off the walls, banging into every piece of furniture in the pitch-black room. The ship continued to pitch in every direction as it tossed her around.

She yanked the door open to find Hades standing in the doorway. His hair was plastered to his head. His eyes were wild as he pulled her to him.

"We need you." He had to scream over the cacophony of noise. Her heart pitched more wildly than the boat at his omission.

"What can I do?" she asked, her voice graveled from her unexpected screams that tore out of her repeatedly throughout the night.

"A mast broke and injured the crew. Cook can't mend them all. I need you to help him. We have them in the dining room. It's not pretty. I trust you can take care of them."

Charlotte wanted to throw her arms around him. He didn't ask if she could do it as if he had all the faith in her.

"Let's go." She moved to walk around him, on a mission to prove his faith in her was not unfounded. He grabbed her tightly before she had made it three steps.

The ship continued its uncoordinated dance as they fell into each other. She wasn't positive who moved first. Their lips collided in a fury the storm couldn't match.

He tasted of salt and she wanted to soak in his essence. The ship rose as their tongues dueled. The tempest outside fueled them to lean on each other as they took their fill. The ship rose and plummeted down, pulling them apart as only the fury of Mother Nature could.

"Be safe." He traced her swollen bottom lip with the pad of his thumb before securing her hat more tightly on her head.

She nodded, unable to speak. The kiss, even though it was only seconds ago, replayed in her mind, making her whole body feel fuzzy. They walked up together, bumping into each other as the ship continued to be tossed around.

"Be safe," she told him as they parted, not knowing what else to say but needing to say something to him.

He nodded at her before running back to the deck in the opposite direction she needed to go. He disappeared in the darkness. The storm had covered what seemed to be the whole ocean. She carefully threaded her way over to the dining hall, weaving around the carnage on the deck. The stench of blood overtook the smell of the pelting rain.

She adjusted her hat and took a fortifying breath before walking into what seemed like the eye of the mayhem. Men, some she recognized and some she didn't, were strewn about the dining room.

Cook caught her eye and motioned for her to come to him. There were lanterns lit around the room, swinging precariously as the storm continued to show her strength.

“Captain said you have healing knowledge.” He didn’t look at her as he sewed the leg of a passed-out sailor.

“I do.” She looked around, assessing what needed to be done just as Agatha taught her to do in these types of situations.

“Tell young Cerberus if you need anything. Keep as many of them alive as you can. Cut off what you need to.” He kicked a medical bag toward her, his focus unwavering on what he was doing.

Charlotte swallowed as the thought of amputating anything brought bile to the top of her throat. She had assisted Agatha in numerous amputations, and she hated every single one of them.

Charlotte beckoned Cerberus as she moved around the injured person, making a mental list of who needed attention first.

“I need you to boil water in the largest pot Cook has. I need you to keep the water boiling until I tell you it’s no longer needed.” Charlotte didn’t wait for Cerb to give her recognition that he’d follow her orders.

A calmness settled over her as she went over to a sailor she knew as Pappi. His arm was a jumbled mess of bone, muscle, and sinew. The bone was protruding above his elbow, and she knew there was no saving it.

"Charlie?" Pappi's forehead was beaded with sweat and blood. She was surprised he hadn't passed out from the pain.

"I'm going to have to cut it off." She said this with no nonsense coating her statement, letting him know there was no room for argument.

"Aye," he answered, his eyes rolling back in his head until he forced them back on her.

"I've done this before. Do you trust me?" They stared at each other as she waited for his reply. She knew she was a feeble cabin boy to Pappi and the rest of them. She needed him to see her unwavering determination and in earning that, she exuded confidence she didn't have.

Pappi finally nodded before leaning over the table and retching all over the floor, barely missing Charlotte's boots.

"Cerb, I need the water now," she shouted over the cacophony of noise. The ship continued to lurch, yet Charlotte was steady, her determination making her sturdy.

Cerb showed up with a smaller basin of water. The larger pot boiled in the corner. Charlotte nodded in approval as she held the laudanum she found in the medical bag over Pappi's face. The older man went slack. Charlotte didn't waste any time.

"Hold what you can below the elbow," Charlotte called over the wind and moaning of the men around her.

"I can't," Cerb cried out, his face a sickly shade of green.

"You can and you will. We need to do this quick so we can get to the others." Charlotte refused to show how unsettled she was with what she was about to do. She pulled the fake calm around her like a comforting blanket. A vision of Hades' arms around her as she slept flickered through her mind before she pushed it away. She needed confidence not softness at the moment.

"Hold his arm, now." Charlotte moved, holding the saw in the fire until it glowed red. She poured alcohol over the wound, set the saw, and began sawing, not paying attention to the sizzling flesh or the smell thrusting itself in her nostrils.

Cerb's hands began to slide off Pappi's arm.

"Do not pass out on me. We have a lot to do tonight."

Cerb leaned over and vomited but didn't move his grasp.

When the arm had been severed and cauterized, Charlotte poured more alcohol on the wound and moved to the next man.

Cerb followed her like a specter. He didn't say a word, only doing as she ordered, with his pale face and shaking limbs.

Charlotte amputated a leg, stitched up numerous wounds, and set a couple breaks with the determination of a seasoned soldier. She didn't falter in what she had to do. She focused on the task until it was done and then went right into the next task.

She hadn't noticed the storm had released its hold on Persephone and she was now calmly rocking toward her destination until she finished sewing a rather nasty head wound.

Charlotte wiped her forehead, walking over to the last patient. Shark glared at her, a cut seeping blood from his forearm.

"Don't touch me. I'll wait for Cook," he grumbled as she neared him.

"Cook is back in the kitchen. He won't be doing any more medical assisting tonight. It's me or nothing." She put her hands on her hips, refusing to allow him to bully her.

When Cook had realized she had everything underhand, he went back into the kitchen to get meals ready for the infirm and the lucky ones who survived the mast break.

"I choose nothing."

Charlotte rolled her eyes as she headed over to him. "That's a nasty cut. Let me at least put a couple of stitches in it."

"I said don't touch me." Shark pushed Charlotte when she got near enough. Her tired limbs didn't catch her in time, and she slipped on the blood and gore coating the floor. She landed on the floor hard, dislodging her hat in the process. Her long braid fell down her back, and Shark grinned, an evil glint in his eyes.

"I knew there was something different about you, Charlie," he sneered.

He moved off the table he'd been waiting on and stalked up to her with a menacing glare. She scrambled to her feet, not wanting to give him any advantage.

"Do you see this? Captain brought a woman on our ship. No wonder the mast broke. There is no reason for a woman to be on a ship. You're bad luck." He threw out his arms, encompassing all the injured who were still on their makeshift table beds.

"Shut up, Shark. There is always a storm this time of year," one of the injured crew that Charlotte had set his broken arm hours ago yelled out. "She fixed all of us without complaint while all you do is bellyache."

"Do you want another broken arm, Shifty?" Shark threatened without moving his furious gaze from Charlotte's.

Shark's arm bled on the floor, the persistent dripping the only noise in the still room.

"And why would Shifty want another broken arm?"

The command in Hades' voice was unmistakable. Charlotte turned slightly, not wanting Shark out of her field of vision.

Hades leaned against the doorjamb. His arms were crossed over his middle as he quirked an eyebrow, waiting for Shark to answer.

"You." Shark pointed his uninjured arm at Hades' lounging form. "You brought a woman on this ship. All of this is your fault for bringing her aboard. You're not fit to man this ship."

Hades continued to lean against the door as if Shark's words weren't the start of a mutiny. "I see. And you're saying the storm was her fault?" Hades didn't move his attention from Shark. "A storm we've dealt with nearly every time we traverse these waters during this month."

"If not the storm, then the mast breaking." Shark shot a dirty look at Charlotte when the rest of the crew remained silent at his declaration.

"You mean the mast you were supposed to check and secure before we left port because we knew this storm was a possibility?"

Charlotte's mouth dropped. Her head snapped toward Shark, no longer keeping him in her periphery.

"You were off with that port doxy. It was your job," an injured sailor whom Charlotte had stitched up confirmed.

"A port doxy. I guess women are to be blamed. Just not this one." Hades glanced at Charlotte before searing Shark with a glare that should have flayed him alive.

Shark moved with the grace of a crazed man. He snatched his sword from its scabbard and pointed it at Charlotte. "It's her fault. I'll not lose all my money on a wench. We're already behind our schedule for the task you had to complete before we left." He jerked his sword, still pointed at Charlotte. "I'm assuming this was the task. The war is almost over. This is our last shipment to the colonies for weapons. I'm not going to let her ruin my money. Do you agree?" He had the room's attention. Charlotte's stomach churned, wondering if his passionate speech turned the men she'd just healed away from her.

"What do you suppose we should do about it?" Hades asked when none of the men spoke up.

"I want her off this boat. Maybe you'll think better with her no longer clogging your senses with her magic," Shark replied, not moving his sword.

"I'm a witch now?" she asked, unable to keep silent any longer. She wasn't going to let this man turn these men against her when she was fully capable to talk in her defense.

"You've done something to mess with the captain's senses," he answered.

"Enough," Hades bellowed. He crossed the large room in long, swift strides. His boots stamped the floor with his fury.

Hades stopped right next to Charlotte. Her heart hammered in her chest, and she was surprised the organ wasn't pushing against her ribs where all could see. Hades slowly slid out his sword, his gaze trained on Shark.

There was a collective gasp from the room. Charlotte was certain hers mingled with the rest of the room.

Then he did the unthinkable. He handed Charlotte the sword. Charlotte's head snapped in his direction as he held out the sword for her to take.

"What are you doing?" she whispered, knowing everyone could hear her with the silence descended around the ship as they watched the events unfold before them.

"Allowing you to show him exactly what he is insulting." He pressed the hilt into her sweaty, blood-soaked hand.

Charlotte wanted to tell him she couldn't, but the words refused to leave the prison of her mouth. As long as Shark sneered in front of her, she would be his target. She refused to allow him to think in any situation, especially the current one, that she wasn't strong enough to handle her own.

Her fingers flexed on the hilt, the metal already drinking in her heat.

"Bored of her already, Captain? Want me to dispatch your plaything? Maybe we should pass her around before getting rid of her."

Charlotte's sword pressed against his throat as the last word left his vile mouth. "I will not be anyone's plaything. Are you done procrastinating or are you going to fight me? I'm sick of hearing the asinine things spewing out of your ignorant mouth." Charlotte flicked the tip of the sword just enough to cause a bead of blood to slip out of his weather-worn neck.

Shark roared at the insult, which was exactly what Charlotte had been counting on. She knew how to fight, yet this man was larger and stronger than her. She needed every advantage she could get if she was going to best him, and she was going to best him.

He thrust his sword toward her without any sense of his attack. Charlotte easily moved out of the way and his momentum caused him to crash into a table. He turned quickly, but Charlotte was ready for him. She had her sword ready and slashed before he had turned. He was fast, though, but she was able to nick his already bleeding arm, making the wound gape even more.

Shark's eyes flashed with hatred, dark and sickly. Charlotte shivered at the intensity of his look, but she also knew he wasn't thinking rationally. And she was going to take advantage of that fact. Their swords clashed over and over again. Her ears were ringing from the constant barrage of metal meeting metal.

The men who were able to move crowded against the wall as they cheered. Charlotte's already aching body hurt with every thrust or counter thrust.

Shark's eyes were glazed over and blood poured down his arm with every movement. Charlotte reminded herself to stay in control. To keep her head, as it was the only advantage she had. She saw a small opening and jabbed her sword into the tattered skin on his arm. He acted as if he didn't feel what had to be excruciating pain. Panic lanced up Charlotte's spine, but she tamped it down.

He lunged, catching her hip, but she blocked the sword before it could cut into skin. Her body screamed at the contact. Charlotte angled her sword to push him away and a miracle happened. The blood coursing down his arm made his sword slip from his grasp. Charlotte immediately pounced and thrust her sword through his wrist as he reached for his weapon, severing his hand completely.

The room went quiet as she held her sword against his throat. With pressure against his neck, she had him on his knees in front of her before he could register his hand was no longer attached.

The room went up in a cheer while she held the sword in place as her muscles screamed with exhaustion. She wouldn't move, though. Her arms would have to fall off for her to relent her position.

"Are you done? I refuse to allow you to sully my reputation, or all women, for that matter, with your insecurities. In fact, you are done." Charlotte pressed her sword where he gagged from the pressure against his windpipe. She wanted this ordeal to be over, but she knew she needed to make a point.

"Do you understand me? You're done." She pressed the sword a second longer before removing it and placing it on her shoulder. The weight almost brought her down to her knees. A strength she shouldn't have possessed kept her up.

Charlotte stepped back, wanting nothing more than a bath and a bed. She would be fine with a floor at the moment, but she needed everyone to see she had prevailed before retreating.

Hades approached her and took the heavy sword from her. She was about to press herself against him, but he continued walking, thankfully stopping the show of weakness.

Charlotte watched in horror as he raised the sword and sliced Shark's head off with one powerful stroke.

Shark's body remained upright as if unaware it had been severed from its head. As if time had slowed, the body slumped to the ground in a leisurely motion. Shark's head stared into the abyss with its eyes wide open.

"Does anyone else want to question me or my choices?" Hades spun, catching everyone's eyes. He had a smirk on his face as his crew shook their heads or shouted, "No, Captain."

"I have delivered on every promise I have given you. We will make this delivery, and you will all have your payment. As Charlotte has stated, we are done. Someone clean this trash up." He kicked the body in front of him for good measure and turned as if looking at Shark's body disgusted him.

Chapter Thirteen

Hades grabbed Charlotte around the waist and propelled her out of the room. Charlotte allowed him to manhandle her down to the room, her body giving up any semblance of having control. Her limbs were shaking by the time he shut the door. The room was bathed in darkness, clouding Charlotte's vision with white dots. She leaned farther into Hades. He lit a lamp on his desk, gathering her close to him.

"You were magnificent," he whispered in her ear. "You are magnificent."

Charlotte lifted her head, her lips grazing his. The gentle, unexpected touch ignited the fire that simmered whenever she was near him. She pressed her lips harder into his, wanting to feel him and only him.

She wanted to banish the blood and pain she'd just been drenched in. She wanted him to erase the sight of Shark's head detaching from his body, only to roll for a second before plopping at its resting place.

Hades cupped the back of her head and devoured her. His tongue thrust into her mouth, claiming every part he could get to. Charlotte met him with the same desperation. She knew this was inevitable.

Hades had penetrated her every thought for weeks now. He flowed in her veins and there was no way to extricate him. She wasn't sure she'd want to if it were a possibility.

Her hands ripped his shirt from his body. He moaned in her mouth when she scraped her nails down his bare chest. Her shirt went the way of his.

"What is this?" He gasped as he noticed the cloth binding her breasts.

"They would have given me away," she answered, her lips finding his again, not wishing to be separated from him. Wishing she could fuse herself to him.

She gasped when cool air hit her uncovered nipples. The pebbled peaks hardened at his touch.

"Much better," he muttered as he kissed down her neck, licking her collarbone.

She arched as he took one of the peaks into his mouth and sucked. Fire burst between her legs as he licked, sucked, and bit her nipples until her knees no longer functioned.

He unlatched from her nipple and carried her to the bed. When she was lying on the mattress, she pushed out her arms to welcome his weight. The dim light caught the blood covering her arms. She drew them back, but he stopped her.

"Don't hide. You were ferocious, protecting my men and your honor. You're bathed in blood because you survived and conquered."

"I was so tired. I didn't know if I would be able to best him," she admitted.

He continued to suckle on her breasts before licking her collarbone, moving to her neck.

When he handed the sword over to her, she felt powerful and in control of her life as she never had. The worry that she would fail was there, skirting the corner of her mind, but only now, after the victory, would she allow herself to admit her fear.

"I had no doubt you would best him. You are the strongest person on this ship."

Charlotte's heart swelled with emotion. She had to bite her tongue to keep it from pushing past her lips.

His knee was on the mattress as he gazed his fill of her chest. Her breast abraded from his attention. Her stomach quivered at the intimacy. With slow, deliberate movements, he unlaced her trousers and pulled them off her legs in one swift, hard yank.

She moved to cross her legs, feeling completely bare and not with just her body at his assessment. He stopped her with his hands on her knees, spreading her wider so he could glimpse the wetness between her legs.

He groaned as he took one finger and traced the sensitive, intimate skin. Charlotte bucked at the touch of the pad of his finger where only he had ever touched.

"So responsive." He lifted his finger and sucked it deep in his mouth, and she swore she could feel it as if he were sucking on her.

He lowered his face after he sucked his finger clean, and panic struck her as his intentions became clear. "What are you..." She didn't finish her sentence as his tongue traced the same path his finger had just traveled.

Her body lifted off the mattress at the foreign sensation. His strong arm snaked under her waist, keeping her hips from touching back down on the mattress, and then he consumed her. His tongue licked as if he were a starving man. Charlotte writhed on the mattress, but his strong arm kept her exactly where he wanted her.

He pushed his tongue deep inside of her and Charlotte moaned loudly at the exquisite feeling. She never imagined this was possible with his mouth.

“Please,” she pleaded, needing more but unable to voice what she needed.

“I’ve got you, Lottie.” Two fingers eased into her wetness and she bucked at the sensation of being stretched by the large digits.

“Yes,” she cried as his tongue went back to assaulting her clitoris in the most delicious way.

“Bloody hell, you taste like sin.” His words ratchet her pleasure, pushing her closer to the edge of something she knew would be earthshattering. “My sin,” he claimed as he took her nub in his mouth and sucked while his tongue circled it slowly but picked up the pace with every revolution.

Charlotte’s legs began to shake as his fingers and tongue brought her closer to an unknown precipice. “I could eat your cunny for every meal.”

He wiggled his fingers, touching something deep inside her, causing her to leap into the void she’d been flirting with. Charlotte cried out as her body bucked and pulsed against his mouth. He continued his assault with his fingers and his mouth, dragging out the pleasure until her body went limp.

He removed his arm from under her and kissed his way back up her body. Goose flesh burst over her heated skin. A fine sheen of sweat coated her as her heart hammered in her chest.

"You're perfect," he told her as he kissed her deeply, letting her taste herself on his lips. The lingering taste of her mingled with him was an aphrodisiac.

Her eyes rolled back in pleasure and absurdity. She had heard the maids gossiping that men would say the silliest things after being intimate, but calling her perfect while she was coated in blood and sweat was ridiculous.

He grabbed her chin, forcing her to listen to him. "You. Are. Perfect." He punctuated each word with a kiss on a different part of her face.

"I'm not." She didn't know why she was arguing with him on this subject, but she didn't want to be seen as perfect. She wanted—no, needed, to be seen as herself, flaws and all. She wanted to be accepted for exactly who she was and the person she would become as she evolved into who she was meant to be.

"You're perfect for me."

Charlotte was shocked to feel tears burning the back of her eyes. His words undid a knot in her heart she hadn't even known was there.

She lifted to kiss him but stopped when she felt scratchy material abrading her sensitive skin. "You're still wearing trousers?"

He smirked as he suckled her breasts. "I wanted to worship you without distraction."

"I want you," she whispered the omission. Inherently knowing he wouldn't go any further unless she explicitly asked for it. Not after what happened the first time.

"I want you," she stated again with more conviction in her voice.

He quirked an eyebrow as he stilled after she whispered her request.

Her heart wanted to jump out of her chest and bury itself into him. He wasn't questioning her; he was waiting for confirmation of what was truly happening.

"I want you. Not for power over my life or my body. I want you, not because I want to verify I'm alive after what we just endured. I want you because my body yearns for you. I want you."

His mouth crashed against hers. She smiled under the intensity of his desire because it matched her frantic need. He leaned to the side, yanking his trousers off as if they offended him with their existence. The renting of the fabric made Charlotte laugh.

"You laugh, but it's not every day a goddess invites you into her bed." He kissed her, wiping the laughter off her face.

Her hands roamed freely over his naked body. The rough hardness was a contradiction to her body. She squeezed his rump in her hand, causing him to pause his quest to decide which breast he favored the most.

"I've wanted to do that for so long," she admitted. "Your arse in those tight trousers as we practice sword play has brought havoc to my mind for weeks," she confessed.

He reached around and squeezed hers with just as much fierceness. "I think I'll burn every dress you own and keep your perfect arse in trousers. Your body was meant to be worshipped."

"Here's your altar." She raised her chest so they were pressed together. "Worship me, Hades."

His eyes went molten. The force of his lips stole her breath as he had already stolen her heart.

"I'm yours, Lottie. I've always been yours. I'm a greedy pirate. I won't give you up. You're mine just as much as I'm yours."

Charlotte's breath faltered. "I should fight someone to the death more often if it gets you to confess like that." She needed to bring some levity to the situation. As the intensity of the room was pressing down on her more than his weight.

He smiled his brilliant smile. "If you're not ready, I will happily feast on you again."

Wetness pooled between her legs as the thought of him licking her again flitted through her mind.

"Later, I want this." She reached between them and wrapped her hand around his thick shaft. Her fingers barely touched as she stroked the heated flesh.

"It's yours, but you need to stop your ministrations before I ruin myself in front of you."

She cocked her head, confused at his statement, and he smiled wider.

"If you continue to touch me, I'll spend myself before I can enter you," he explained.

His hand stroked her between her thighs, the wetness making noise when he pushed two fingers inside of her. "Lottie," he sighed as he removed his fingers and licked them clean.

He positioned his shaft in her entrance, and she felt the pressure of the wide tip press into her. She held her breath, waiting for the intrusion.

"This won't hurt like last time." The muscles in his neck strained as if he were refraining from thrusting into her.

That wouldn't do. Charlotte grasped his firm buttocks and pushed her hips up, thrusting him all the way to the hilt. Charlotte cried out and he stilled, fully seated inside of her.

"Did I hurt you?"

She shook her head, filling full as she accepted all of him, but it wasn't uncomfortable as it was the first time.

"Please, don't be gentle. Make me yours."

He groaned as he pulled out until the tip was poised at her entrance before thrusting back in. Charlotte's body felt as if fire were burning her from the inside out. Hades moved with some force, but she could tell he was still holding back.

On his next thrust, she pushed into the mattress, meeting him in the middle. The sound of their skin slapping together was an aphrodisiac she wasn't expecting.

"I said, make me yours," she commanded as she continued to meet his thrusts.

Hades chuckled in a dark, seductive way as he slid off the bed, bringing her with him. He grasped her hips, lining her up to his rigid erection, and slammed into her. His feet planted on the ground and his hands lifted her where he wanted her. The bed groaned from the force, but Charlotte groaned louder.

He pounded into her, dominating her. Claiming her. Charlotte cried out as his pelvic bone grazed her sensitive nub.

Charlotte clawed at the blankets before grasping her breasts in her hand. His eyes tracked her movement as she squeezed her breasts before pinching her nipples.

The guttural groan he released made her clench around him. Hades continued to thrust into her as she stimulated her breasts, both of them panting and groaning at the ecstasy they were surrendering to.

He wrapped his arm around her hips as his other hand began circling her clitoris in easy passes. As he intensified his pressure on her sensitive nub, he thrust harder.

"Let go for me, Lottie," he pleaded.

Charlotte's eyes focused on her name branded over his heart and let go. Her body clenched, and all of her muscles seized before breaking in a wave that rivaled Mother Nature. Her walls clenched and pulsed around Hades as he lost all control and moved into her with swift thrusts. His jaw was clenched as he locked eyes with her.

"Let go for me, Hades."

He groaned loudly. His eyes went wide as she felt him release inside of her, filling her with his essence. They stayed locked together, him standing on the floor, Charlotte propped up with his arm under her hips. Not yet ready to part.

"You were right. You definitely did not do it right the first time."

Hades' mouth swung open before he burst into a loud belly laugh that brushed her sensitive nub. She scrambled away, unable to handle the friction his laughter caused.

"Where are you going?" He leaned down, licking around her belly button, causing the fire she thought was banked to come roaring back to life.

"I'm sensitive," she admitted as he kissed her stomach and hip bones.

"Ahh." He pulled out of her, and she felt bereft from the loss of him.

He climbed on the bed, bringing her with him. She slithered over the blankets, her body weightless and sated. Hades pulled her against him, cocooning her in his arms and legs as he maneuvered the blankets over both of them.

She sighed when his fingers interlaced with hers. She admired the strength of his hands wrapped around hers and was proud that her hands portrayed strength as well.

"Get some sleep, Goddess. I have plans for you when you're rested."

She shivered as his words caressed her neck. "You get some sleep, Pirate. I have plans of my own."

He chuckled, raising the hair on the back of her neck. "I'm all yours."

She stiffened before melting back into the strength and security of his chest. "I'm all yours."

There, she had said it. They both knew it to be true. This man, Jack, Hades, was the one she wanted. The only one she needed.

He shifted behind her, lifting her leg and pulling it over his hip before sliding into her. His teeth bit into the back of her neck as he gently moved. Charlotte squeezed her fingers into his as they moved in a silent acceptance of their confession.

Her release built slowly as he moved leisurely behind her, his hand rubbing her clitoris. This lovemaking was different, yet the crescendo was as powerful as the first. Her stomach clenched from the force of it. Hades cursed behind her as his own release followed hers. They lay together, tangled and filthy from the night's events. Connected in the most primal way as they both succumbed to sleep, which beckoned for them to follow.

Charlotte woke, warm and sheltered in Hades' arms. She snuggled into his chest, wishing for the sun to leave, allowing them their reprieve to last a little bit longer. Hades chuckled behind her, kissing the back of her neck.

“As much as I’d enjoy worshipping you, I need to ensure the ship is still afloat.” He kissed the back of her neck, nibbling on the place where he seemed to particularly love biting.

His hand slid down her belly and Charlotte halted his progress. “If you go any further, we will not be leaving his room.”

“Let the ship sink.”

“Captain, that doesn’t sound at all like the infamous pirate, Hades.”

She moaned as his finger grazed over the sensitive skin.

“It does when he has the one thing he’s ever wanted for himself in his bed.” As his finger stroked her, Charlotte opened her legs, giving him better access.

She reached behind her to grasp his length that he was currently prodding her with. Right before her fingers enclosed over the engorged flesh, there was a loud knock.

Chapter Fourteen

Hades growled from behind her. “I’ll kill them.”

“Cap’in, Cook sent me down here for your bath. Said you would need it after—”

“All right, Cerb,” Hades interrupted before the young boy could finish what he was going to say.

Charlotte buried her face in his arm to stifle the giggle. She could only imagine the descriptive words Cook had used to describe what they had been doing. Charlotte was mortified when she realized the whole ship would be privy to their escapades.

“Don’t fret, Goddess. You screamed my name so loud Poseidon himself knows where your loyalty lies.”

Charlotte felt her cheeks redden as she cleared her scratchy throat, which had been abused last night from all the screaming he’d just mentioned. Hades chuckled as he climbed over her, kissing her cheek as he pulled on his trousers. He glared down at them as half his upper thigh was exposed from the large rip they'd gained last night in his haste to get them off.

Charlotte threw her head back and laughed. She felt free and sore in all the right places. Hades grinned at her as he retrieved another pair of trousers and tossed her one of his large shirts. Charlotte scrambled to put it on, feeling every bit of activity she did yesterday.

Cerb grinned as he hauled in the first bucket of water.

"Eyes to yourself," Hades commanded with more authority than Charlotte felt was necessary.

"Sorry, Cap'in. Sorry, Charlie. I mean Charlotte." Cerb's ears turned bright red as he averted his eyes and focused on his task.

When Cerb finished dumping the last of the water, he scurried away from Hades' scrutinizing gaze.

Charlotte laughed, smacking him on the chest. "You didn't have to stare at him like that."

"Like what?"

"As though you were going to unleash vengeance on his ancestors and future children while he was pouring your bathwater, I might add."

Hades snatched her hand as she was pulling it away. He placed small kisses on each of her fingertips, making her toes curl against the wood floor.

"He needs to know, Lottie."

He held her stare this time and all the vengeance was wiped from his face, but the force was undeniable as to what he was trying to convey.

She held his stare right back, showing that she understood and she did. If any woman were to slide glances at Hades, although she would understand and not blame the woman for Hades was a magnificent man, she would also want to make it known he was only available to stare at from afar and nothing more.

"You're it, Charlotte. You're everything I've been looking for on land or on the sea."

She leaned up and kissed him lightly on the lips as she swallowed down the emotions clogging her throat.

"You're the safety I've searched for in order for me to become what I was meant to be. Thank you for giving me that freedom."

He pressed his forehead to hers and they soaked each other's essence until it was carved into their bone marrow.

"Let's get in the bath before all the hard work Cerb had to do to bring us hot water is for naught." He helped her out of his shirt and washed her from the tips of her toes to the ends of her hair.

She was expecting his hands to wander, but once again he did what she least expected and took care of her. He washed all the blood off her body, scrubbing her scalp until it tingled. When he felt she was sufficiently clean, he pulled her out of the tub, wrapped her in a towel, and set her on the bed to warm up.

Although she had to admit watching him as he cleaned himself warmed her up more than any blanket could. Unable to stay still, Charlotte dropped the towel and walked over to him. His eyes went black with lust as she kneeled down and skimmed the relinquished soap over his delectable body. He groaned when she washed his hair, scraping her nails over his scalp.

When they were both clean, they stood, taking each other in. Both had wet hair dripping down their backs and pruned fingertips, but neither could look away.

"I'm in heaven," he told her, bringing her in close to his body and holding her tightly.

"Why, Hades, I assumed you would be in hell." She leaned down, lifted the towel, and pulled the head of his fast-growing cock into her mouth. He groaned as his fingers tangled in her hair. She sucked hard until the tip hit the back of her throat. His finger clenched in her wet tresses as she swallowed around his length before popping it out of her mouth and walking toward her clothes.

He let out a groaned chuckle. "Hell, it is. I will return the torture. Have no doubt about that."

Charlotte shivered at the threat.

In order to keep their wandering hands to themselves, they pulled on their clothes from opposite sides of the room.

"That is a travesty," Hades said as he watched her bind her breasts in cloth.

She blew him a kiss, still not trusting either of them to get near each other. When they were dressed, they held hands as they made it up to the top deck.

Charlotte was shocked at what she saw when she emerged on deck. The mast was billowing in the wind as if it hadn't wreaked havoc on the sailors who depended on it. The deck was scrubbed, and everyone was hard at work as if they hadn't gone through a man-eating storm.

"Mornin', Captain. Mornin', Charlie," was issued from numerous sailors as they walked toward the kitchen. The hint of smiles and mischief in their voices was obvious.

Charlotte's mouth twitched as they all made sure to give her a knowing look. A sly glance toward Hades showed he was having a hard time keeping a straight face as well.

"Get back to work or I'll make you all stay on board when we dock and save your money instead of spending it on all the port doxies."

They groaned. "You would deny us what you're getting?" one of the braver sailors shouted out in the crowd so as not to be easily identified.

Charlotte blushed but knew she needed to do something so they wouldn't lose respect for her. "Ahh, you see, boys, the captain doesn't have to pay for it."

The ship went silent, and Charlotte's eyes went wide as her palm began to sweat in Hades', wondering if she'd ventured on the wrong route.

Boisterous laughter rang out on the ship and Hades squeezed her hand to let her know he approved.

"She's a keeper, Captain."

Hades glanced at her quickly, but the smoldering look he gave her made her feel as if he had stared at her for longer. "She is, and her name is Lady Charlotte. Treat her as if her happiness determines how much you'll get paid at the end of this voyage. Because it does. Now let's get to the colonies so we can get our money."

A loud cheer went out through the crew as they made their way toward the kitchen. A flurry of work happened around Charlotte as the crew made sure the lost time would be made up for.

Cook smiled and wrapped Charlotte in a hug when they entered the kitchen. "I knew you were special. You saved those men's lives last night, Charlotte. These men owe you everything."

Charlotte took in a large gulp of air when the huge man let her go as he had knocked most of the air in her lungs out when he'd wrapped her in his arms.

Her eyes stung and she wasn't sure if it was from the loss of air or Cook's words. Cook placed a heaping plate of food in front of her and slapped her on the back, knocking the breath she'd just gained back right back out of her lungs.

Hades grinned as he bit into a warmed biscuit. Charlotte shot him a glare before stuffing food into her mouth. She was famished, and she remembered she hadn't had food since the storm started, even though Cook had sent her down with a bag. Her stomach had been too far lodged in her throat to eat anything, and so the food in the quarters still remained.

After they had their fill of food, Hades led her to the top deck, where he went over everything that had happened while they were sleeping. She blushed deeply when Jackal mentioned how long they had slept the morning away.

Cerb came bounding up and Charlotte took over his lessons while Hades and Jackal spoke. When Cerb became jittery, Charlotte brought out the daggers, and they sparred. Cerb gave her more respect after hearing what had happened with Shark.

The day was beautiful as if the aftermath of the storm didn't exist to the peaceful ocean. The sea was the darkest blue she'd ever seen, and the sky was the opposite, a clear blue with white puffy clouds dotting the horizon. Charlotte's arms shook after sparring with Cerb faster than they normally did. Her fatigue was evident in her waning strength. The extent of everything she had done the night before took its toll.

Hades must have noticed her fatigue. "Are you ready to fight with me?" he asked, taking Cerb off guard, and Charlotte poked him lightly with her dagger.

"Yes, Captain," Cerb answered joyfully, not even noticing Charlotte had won a point based on the rules Hades had given them.

Charlotte leaned against the railing as she watched a jubilant Cerb listen to Hades' as if he were giving him the key to life, and maybe he was.

An angry yowl had her glancing down. A large orange tabby cat, with one eye and half its left ear, stared at her, yowling again.

"You must be Cassiopeia. I can tell why you're Hades' favorite girl." Charlotte leaned down and met the mangy cat as she wound her large body through her legs.

"I see you met Cassiopeia," Hades stated as he dodged Cerb's thrust.

"I should have destroyed more than your pillows, Captain." She smiled at him as she continued to pet the feline. "She was worth at least a couple smashed plates as well."

Hades laughed as Charlotte's face heated, remembering the jealous assault she had succumbed to when she thought Cassiopeia was a woman.

Her eyes grew heavy as the sun heated her back, making her muscles feel languid. Cassiopeia curled around her feet, a loud purr running up her legs.

"Here, Lady Charlotte."

Charlotte jolted, not realizing she had started to nod off.

Jackal smiled at her as he set a stool next to her feet. "We wouldn't want you falling overboard."

"Thank you." Charlotte sat down, grateful to get off her feet. She knew she had worked a lot the last night but hadn't counted on how everything that had happened would affect her body.

She tried to stay awake as Hades, with his firm patience, taught Cerb, but with the sun and the rhythmic rocking of the ship, she never had a chance. Charlotte startled when her body was lifted.

"It's me." Hades calmed her as he held her close to his chest. Charlotte snuggled into his hard chest, not bothering to open her eyes. She sighed when he placed her on the bed and undid the laces on her boots. "I should have given you a day off from practice."

Charlotte wasn't too exhausted. She didn't miss the worry in Hades' voice. She cracked her eyes open and saw him standing over her, his face filled with concern.

"You will not treat me as if I'm made of spun glass, Pirate. We just had the conversation where I told you how much I appreciate you letting me grow into who I'm supposed to be, and even though I'm not exactly sure who that is, I am positive a weak woman is not what I'm meant to be."

The concern was washed from his face at her words. "You are correct, Goddess, but even if you weren't my reason for living and instead you were one of the men up there"—he pointed to the ceiling, indicating the deck—"I would also make them go easy, being that you not only practiced becoming a pirate, but you also weathered your first storm, amputated and stitched men throughout the night, bested the scourge of my ship, and then received numerous climaxes under my hand, tongue, and other appendages."

Charlotte batted his chest at his crude words, but her movements had no force behind them. She wasn't sure if that was due to being exhausted or she secretly enjoyed the harsh talk.

"Hush, you filthy pirate."

"Your filthy pirate." He kissed her nose. "Get some rest. I have more plans for you tonight."

"More plans," she teased as she rolled over on her side, sleep dragging her under.

"Sleep, Lottie."

Charlotte opened her mouth to protest, but a yawn took over. She listened as Hades righted the chair she'd wedged under the desk and sat, pulling out parchment. The sound of him scratching notes lulled her to sleep.

Chapter Fifteen

"It's time to wake up." Hades' voice pulled her from a deep sleep.

She wrapped her arms around him and yanked him on top of her. "Wake me up then, dirty pirate."

After Hades had ensured she was fully awake, they headed to the dining hall. Hades gripped her hand as he led her to the front of the table. An ornate chair sat next to his, waiting for her to grace it with her presence.

She glanced at Hades and saw his jaw was tight. He had trimmed his beard while she was sleeping, pronouncing the aggravated movement. She wondered if he was still worried about her acceptance of him. She stood taller, pushing her shoulders back, showing him how proud she was to be next to him. He pulled out her chair and she sat with the regalness of a queen.

"Thank you, Pirate."

"Thank me later," he whispered back as he settled in next to her.

"I guess we won't be introducing young Charlie to Ida when we get to port," Pappi said, his mouth spread wide in a grin, his missing limb not stopping him from shoveling food in his mouth.

The whole room exploded into laughter as Charlotte shook her head, a small smile on her face. "It saves you from embarrassment when she would have chosen me over the lot of you."

Charlotte laughed so hard her cheeks were aching as the men teased her and each other relentlessly. After dinner was cleaned up, Charlotte and Hades went outside to the deck to watch the stars.

The sailors meandered about, some sitting in a small circle as they talked. A sailor named Mouse pulled out his fiddle and they started singing.

There once was a barkeep his name was Nick and every night, he'd play with his

Fiddle in the moonlight for the lady next door, and if you all saw her, you'd call her

A fine young lady she walked with some pluck

She promised the barkeep a new way to

Raise fine children taught the girls how to knit

The boys are in the back shoveling

Oats and barley they're doing quite well

If you don't like my story, you can go straight to

Sleep.

Charlotte had tears streaming down her face as she listened to the raucous songs and stories the crew told. When the bottle of rum was handed to her, she took a mighty swig, thinking it was similar to the ratafia she had during the holidays.

She spat the horrid liquor out before she could swallow it. It was worse than the liquor her father would imbibe on. Cassiopeia meowed her annoyance loudly and stalked off, no longer lying near Charlotte's feet as she had started to do at least once a day.

"Come on, Lady Charlotte. It will put hair on your chest," Mouse told her as the rest of the crew laughed at her reaction.

She wanted to scrape her tongue with something to get the lingering taste out of her mouth. Hades pulled her on his lap, and when the jug came back to her, she lifted it and swallowed.

Her nose ran and her throat burned with the searing, disgusting alcohol, but everyone who was near watched and she felt the liquor was a test. As much as she wanted to, she didn't show any emotion. After the fourth time, the swill wasn't as hard to swallow.

Charlotte leaned against Hades as she listened to him talk about one of the sea fights he'd been in. He had the crew in rapt attention. The rumble of his words lulled her to sleep.

When he lifted her up, she didn't jerk awake, knowing this time who was carrying her. Also, her head seemed to weigh more than it did that morning.

When Hades laid her on the bed, the urge to laugh hit Charlotte and she giggled.

"Oh, Goddess, it seems you are not perfect. You can't hold your liquor."

His words hit her in the giggles, and she laughed even harder.

"You are going to hate life tomorrow."

Through her laughter, she gasped. "How can I hate tomorrow? I found you. You're mine and I'm yours. Tomorrow is going to be wonderful."

Hades brushed her hair as she continued to giggle. The strokes of his brush stopped her giggling and Charlotte slumped against him, fast asleep.

Evil light seared into Charlotte's eyes. She groaned as she pulled the pillow over her head. The small motion made her want to retch.

"I told you that you would hate today."

Even though she couldn't see him, Charlotte knew he had a self-satisfied smirk on his face.

"If you keep talking so loudly, I'm going to hate you, Pirate. And I'll never divest my clothing for you again." Charlotte's tongue stuck to the top of her mouth and her head pounded as she attempted to threaten him.

"Here." A glass was pushed into Charlotte's hand.

When she moved, her stomach revolted and she rushed to the basin to empty it. With every heave, Charlotte was waiting for her head to explode open. When she had nothing left and was dry heaving into the full basin, Hades carried her to the bed. She drank the water he'd offered her and they both waited to see if her stomach would reject it.

Hades handed her a slice of toasted biscuit and Charlotte nibbled it while she sipped the water. Her eyes felt swollen, and her body ached more than it had the day before.

"Leave me here to die," she said as Hades checked on her, his maps spread out on the desk as if he planned to stay in the room with her as she suffered.

"Why would I do that now that I have you back in my life?"

"Because, Pirate, I'm no good. I will never be normal again."

He chuckled and she gave him a small smile. "There you are, Goddess. You will survive."

Charlotte stayed in bed most of the day. Hades would check on her occasionally after she convinced him to go on deck. Cerb brought in hot water for her to wash up when she was able to move without retching.

"Never drink, Cerb," she warned him as she washed her face, starting to feel some semblance of life.

"You'll get used to it," Cerb consoled her before leaving her.

Charlotte climbed back into bed, resting her head on the headboard as she listened to the ocean slap the side of the ship. The relaxing sound soothed what was left of the headache she had.

"She lives," Hades exclaimed when he walked in and saw her plaiting her hair.

"Hush, Pirate, your voice is still too loud."

He chuckled and kissed the side of her neck. "Would you like to come up and get some air?"

"Yes, please."

Hades led Charlotte up the steps. When they got closer to the top, she squared her shoulders, not wanting to appear weak. She knew the crew was aware she was in her cups the night before, but she wanted them to see that she could recover quickly. She refused to relinquish the respect she had fought so hard to obtain.

“There she is,” Hades muttered as they came up to the deck as she held her head high.

The crew that noticed her first smirked. Some of them chuckled at her unsteady feet.

“Get back to work,” she ordered them before Hades could open his mouth to give them what she assumed was the same command.

With some lighthearted banter, the crew got back to work as Hades led her to the wheel where Jackal was glancing through a spyglass.

“What’s he doing?” she asked, seeing the rigid line of Jackal’s large shoulders.

Hades exhaled deeply. “He has a feeling.”

Charlotte looked at him questioningly.

“Jackal has a sense of things that are to come. He said he’s had an itchy feeling in between his shoulder blades all day.”

Charlotte was about to make a snarky remark, but Hades wasn’t smiling as she thought he would at Jackal’s feelings.

“One thing you should have figured out by now, Goddess, is us sailors are a suspicious lot.”

Charlotte shivered at the harshness of his voice.

“Is it because I’m onboard?”

He quirked his eyebrow at her.

"You know," she prompted when he continued to stare, "because I'm a woman."

"You're not a woman, you're a goddess, and the bad luck left all of their minds when you stitched them up and saved Pappi. This is something different. They respect you, but they also respect Jackle's premonitions."

Charlotte smiled at the thought of her swarthy pirate family accepting her.

Jackal nodded at them when they appeared. "I'm going to go up on the crow's nest, Captain. Keep an eye out."

Jackal didn't wait for Hades to give him permission or to ask him questions. The liveliness that had infected the group after the storm dissipated as Jackal's worry blanketed the ship.

After a week of the ship being under Jackal's cautious inkling, everyone was on edge. Charlotte and Hades slunk away after dinner, not wanting to sulk with the rest of the crew. Hades was needed on deck every couple hours as they were still being vigilant. Jackal's hunches had saved the ship numerous times, according to the crew when they sat around talking after dinner.

"Checkmate," Charlotte crowed as she took Hades' king.

"You cheated." Hades shook his head as he studied the board.

“I did not. You’re too busy protecting your queen, and you forget the king is who you should be watching over.”

Hades stared at her over the board, his eyes molten. “If the queen is gone, there is no point in the king living,” he stated.

Charlotte’s heart sped up at the meaning of his words. She moved over, sat on his lap, wrapped her arms around his neck, and kissed him all over his face.

“I love you, Pirate.”

He chuckled as she continued pressing kisses over his cheek, forehead, and eyes. She loved it when he was lighthearted, especially after the week of constantly looking over their shoulders.

“Why, Goddess, I think that is the first time you ever admitted you love me.”

She stopped kissing him, waiting for him to return the sentiment. They had never actually spoken the words out loud, and she was more than ready to hear them.

He picked up the queen and rolled it around in his fingers as she began fidgeting on his lap.

“It was a slip of the tongue, Pirate.” She moved to get off his lap, but he anchored her there with his strong arm.

“Last night might have been a slip of the tongue, but I don’t think you telling me you love me was anything but the truth.”

"Well, if you keep smirking at me, I'm going to take it back." Charlotte wanted to smack the face she had just been littering kisses all over moments ago.

Hades gave one of his rare, hearty laughs, set down the queen, and grasped her face in both hands. He began peppering kisses over her face, wiping her scowl away, replacing it with a smile she couldn't hide.

"Lottie, I don't love you."

Charlotte bristled at his words, confused by the juxtaposition of his actions.

"I adore you with my whole being. Love is too small of a word to encompass what I feel for you. You own me in every sense of the word. You are my queen, and I will protect you at all costs."

"You infernal pirate," she said, refusing to cry at his words. "I feel the same."

"Good. I've always fancied being someone's queen."

Charlotte laughed as she snuggled into his chest.

"If I didn't have to be on deck ten minutes ago, I would show you just how much I love you. Especially your body." He squeezed her rump before setting her away from him. "I need to get away from you, or I'll let Jackal run the ship into the ground and not care a wit."

Charlotte pecked him on the lips before moving out of his way.

"I won't be coming back until late. We are moving through choppy waters as we get closer to the colonies. Get some sleep and don't kill my pillows while I'm gone."

"As long as your pillows don't talk back, they'll survive another night."

Hades kissed her on the nose before walking out of the room. Charlotte tossed and turned, not able to sleep without Hades lulling her to sleep. Frustrated, she dressed quickly and pulled on Hades' wool jacket, then put on the hat she rarely wore anymore now that the crew knew she was a woman. On an impulse, Charlotte snatched the queen piece Hades had been fiddling with and stuffed it in the pocket of her trousers, patting the talisman as she headed toward the deck.

"Evening, Charlotte," Pappi called out when he saw her making her way toward Hades.

"Evening, Pappi. How are you feeling?"

Pappi had recovered remarkably well from his amputation. He swore it was the sea water running through his veins that healed him quickly.

"Perfectly well, thanks to you."

Charlotte patted him on the shoulder before moving on. Many of the crew greeted her and by the time she made it to Hades, she was smiling, feeling as if she had finally found her family.

"Lottie, what are you doing out here?" He pulled her in between the large wooden steering wheel and his warm body.

Charlotte leaned back as he held on, not allowing the unruly ocean to steer them off course. Trusting Hades, she looked up at the night sky, mesmerized by the millions of blinking stars.

"It's beautiful out here. I thought the night sky at the country estate was brilliant, but it can't compare to the night sky out here. It's peaceful."

Hades hummed into her hair, his chest rumbling as he wordlessly agreed with her.

"Are you happy, Charlotte?"

She stiffened at the worry in his voice, surprised he would even have to ask that after they had confessed their love for each other.

"I am very happy. I feel content being with you and the crew has been nothing but cordial to me. I know it's because they are terrified of you, but I feel respected and safe here. Which is the first time in my life."

"They aren't terrified of me. They're terrified of you. They know you can weld a needle, a saw, and a sword with ease. You, Goddess, are a force to be reckoned with and they respect you as my queen. You won't regret me, will you? Because as I said, you are mine and I don't let what's mine go."

"I could never regret you. You are my home."

"You're not upset you didn't get to marry old, wrinkly ballocks?"

Charlotte laughed and pushed into him. "Well, I figure someday soon you'll have wrinkly pirate ballocks and I'm patient enough to wait for the day."

They both laughed quietly, not wanting to break the peacefulness of the night with boisterous laughter. They stayed that way for hours, content in each other's arms as Hades steered the ship to their destination.

"What happens after you unload this shipment? And why is this cargo so important to the crew? They seem like this is different from your other shipments." Her eyes blurred, the stars she'd been admiring now a massive glob of blinking light as she relaxed further into Hades.

Hades pulled her closer into his chest as he took a large breath. Charlotte felt his chest expand against her back, her body undulating with the movement.

"This will be the last shipment we bring to the colonies. The war is theirs if they don't overextend their hands. The seas are getting too dangerous to keep sending cargo over there. Mostly because of the trouble we've been having with the Royal Navy as they get desperate to hold onto what little control they have left. We are charging triple our normal rate."

"Triple? You are a dirty pirate."

He chuckled and she loved that she could feel the movement on her back.

"I'm your dirty pirate, Goddess. And yes, triple our normal fee will allow the crew to retire into a life of luxury if they'd like. Some have decided to stay in the colonies and start a new life there. This is the end to a lot of pirate careers."

"What are your plans for after?" She wasn't worried about his answer. He had committed himself to her, and their relationship was the most stable one she'd ever had.

"You mean, what are our plans after?"

She turned her head and grinned at him. "Yes, what will we do after this is over?"

He grasped her by the waist and twirled her around, returning her grin. "Whatever you want, Lottie. The world is ours. I have amassed a fortune, which is at your disposal. We can sail the world. We can retire on the English estate I have."

Still lifted into the air, she looked down at him and laughed. "You have an English estate?"

He lowered her, letting her body slide delectably down his. "We have an English estate that I won in a card game with an overeager Earl who was too far into his cups to care."

"You took it?" she asked in astonishment.

"If he is careless enough to gamble his unentitled family estate away, then he didn't deserve it. So yes, I took it, and now we own it."

"Dirty Pirate," she muttered, kissing the tip of his nose.

"So, what shall it be, Lottie Love?"

Charlotte's heart skipped as she stared up at Hades.

"I don't know, Dirty Pirate. As long as I'm with you. Let's get your cargo safely to the colonies and decide after you secure your payment."

"Perfect."

He kissed her under the moonlit stars, the ocean slapping against the side of the ship. This should have been the perfect moment, but Jackal's apprehension made her worried this wouldn't last. After all, everything she had that was perfect was always taken away.

He must have noticed her inattentiveness to the kiss because he pulled back. His finger stroked her cheek, worry evident on his face.

"What is it, Lottie?"

She shook her head, blinking back tears she didn't realize she was holding back. "Nothing. I think I'm letting Jackal get to me."

"He has gotten to all of us. The stories you've heard are true. Jackal has saved the ship numerous times, and his worry is not to be taken lightly. We'll get through whatever comes our way."

Charlotte couldn't keep the tears at bay. They tracked down her cheeks, the icy ocean air making them cool as they gathered at her chin.

"I'm worried this is happening because of me."

"No, Lot, don't think like that."

"Well, you know women are bad luck on ships," she tried to joke, but it felt flat as the tears continued to fall.

"You are anything but bad luck. Tell me what you're really feeling."

"Nothing good ever stays." She wanted to slap herself for how pathetic she sounded. "That was disgusting. Don't listen to me. I was just in a melancholy mood, and I'm past it now. I no longer allow my future to be dictated by anything or anyone but me."

"Lot, you're allowed to have feelings. You have had awful things happen to you, and I abhor that you have those worries lurking in the back of your head. I promise to commit the rest of my life to banishing those feelings."

Charlotte brushed her lips lightly over his. "My life changed when you wrapped me up in that rug and took me away from that sham of a wedding. I'm now in control of my life and it's because of you."

He kissed her. There wasn't any heat in the kiss, just a mutual agreement that they were in the chaos of life together no matter what their future had in store for them.

Now, if Jackal would get the same thought in his head, everything would be perfect.

Chapter Sixteen

"Come on, Goddess, I want to show you something." Hades had a wide smile on his face when Jackal took the wheel.

It had been two days since Charlotte and Hades confessed their life journeys under the stars. The apprehension on the ship hadn't lifted. Hades and Charlotte decided to play chess more often than being with the crew.

Charlotte couldn't help but smile at Hades. His mood away most of the concern she'd been harboring. Charlotte's worry ratcheted right back when Hades led her to the mast.

She pulled back when he led her to the rungs leading to the crow's nest. The extremely high up crow's nest.

"I'm not going up there," Charlotte whispered, not wanting the crew to overhear the panic in her voice.

"You're not scared, are you, Goddess?"

"Yes, yes, I am, Pirate."

He kissed her deeply. When she melted into his hard chest, he pulled away. "I'll protect you. Remember this is the new Charlotte. Goddess Lottie, if you will."

Charlotte wanted to stick out her tongue and stamp her feet at his argument. "If I fall, I will haunt you for the rest of your life and beyond."

"I wouldn't want it any other way. We're together until we're ghosts and beyond if I have any say in it." He kissed her again as he tied the rope around her waist, which was supposed to save her if she fell. The thought made her want to vomit. He smacked her rump as she took hold of the first rung.

"Get up there, Goddess."

Charlotte's palms were sweaty, and her body had tiny tremors under her skin as she pulled herself up rung after rung. Her muscles shook when she finally reached the top and pushed open the hatch.

Hades pulled himself up as soon as she cleared the way. She sat on the floor of the bucket, curling her whole being around itself. Her body shook from the intensity of the climb and the thought of being so far above deck. The movement of the ship emphasized just how high up they were, making bile rise up Charlotte's throat.

"You're missing it, Lottie." Hades held out his hand to her and Charlotte slowly placed her hand into his. "I've got you, Lot."

Charlotte's knees felt weak as she stood and pressed herself against Hades' muscular body as he held her tightly. Her eyes were closed, and she wanted to turn into Hades' chest instead of looking the way he had her pointed. She wasn't ready to view the vastness of the ocean at this height, and she didn't care if that alone made her a coward.

"Open your eyes, Goddess. I want to give you the world."

Charlotte opened her eyes at his urging and sucked in a shocked breath. It was stunning. The ocean stretched for what seemed like forever. The sun was slowly sinking into the sea, and she wondered if the water was boiling where the sun met the water.

The colors were extraordinary and there were hues she didn't think she'd ever seen before in her life. Everything was on display as if painted just for them.

"It's perfect," she whispered, not wanting to shatter the moment with her voice.

"You're perfect," he answered.

"Pirate, you can do better than that." She smiled as he wrapped himself even tighter around her, pulling her so she was flush against him.

His lips grazed the shell of her ear. "You are perfect for me. Your strength, your resilience, your heart, your body." His hand snuck under her shirt, and he fondled her breast, pinching her nipple. "Especially, your breasts, and your rear." He pushed into her, letting Charlotte feel the hard length of his erection pressing into her.

"You're perfect yourself, Pirate." She moved to turn so she could kiss him, but he stopped her.

"Stay where you are. Enjoy the view. I certainly will."

His hand squeezed her breast as he kissed the back of her neck. Charlotte shivered from the touch. His tongue peeked out and licked the sensitive area before sucking on her earlobe.

A rush of cold air brushed against her backside before his heat replaced the frigid air. Charlotte was shocked when she noticed he had pushed down her trousers without her grasping what he was doing. She'd been so lost in the sensations he'd been giving her from kissing and sucking on her neck she hadn't paid any attention to what his other hand was doing.

"What are you doing?" she asked in a breathless tone.

"Oh, Lottie." His fingers brushed over her sensitive wetness, and she sucked in a breath at the sensation of his warm finger in contrast with the cold wind.

His finger left her and before she could turn, his hands landed on her waist, keeping her put. "Put your hands on the edge."

Charlotte did as she was ordered. She was stunned when he spread her legs and buried his face in between them. She cried out at the unexpected assault. She refused to be embarrassed, or even wonder if the crew could hear her so high up. Hades' finger speared her in one thrust as he continued to lick and suck her as the sun painted the canvased sky in front of her. Charlotte's legs shook as he pulled his fingers out and slowly pushed them back inside as his tongue swirled around her clit. Her knuckles were white from the grip she had on the worn wood.

"Come for me," he ordered her into her wetness. The command sent her spiraling. Her knees buckled from the ferocity of her orgasm as he latched onto her pulsing bundle of nerves. She dug her fingers into the wood to keep her upright, but when Hades moved from between her legs, she sank to the floor.

Hades grabbed her and kissed her deeply as she tasted her release on his lips. Charlotte's muscles were lax, her body liquid from the terror of the climb and the orgasm he'd just milked out of her. After kissing him deeply, until she felt the stirring of passion, Charlotte had an idea.

"Stand up, Pirate. Hands on the edge."

Hades' eyebrow quirked up, but he followed her direction. Charlotte pushed until she could fit in between the wall of the nest and Hades' hardened body.

“Goddess?” he asked, his voice husky as if he were hoping she was going to do what she had planned, but not certain.

“Hush, Pirate, it’s my turn.” Charlotte lowered his trousers and his length sprang out.

Charlotte giggled. “Eager, Pirate?”

“More than you’ll ever know.”

Charlotte sent a tentative lick over the swollen head of his cock. He groaned and she was certain she heard the weathered wood creak under his hands.

Charlotte licked the tip until she was familiar with the texture. With a shuddering breath, she took the tip in her mouth and sucked.

“Goddess,” he moaned. She wasn’t sure if it was a plea or a request.

She sucked deeper until his cock pushed down the back of her throat as she swallowed him down. She wrapped her hand around the length she couldn’t fit as saliva pooled around his thickness. With a swallowing motion, she let the back of her throat massage his cock as she moaned around him.

He groaned louder. Tears tracked down Charlotte’s cheek as she went slowly up and down his shaft. One of his hands tangled in her hair as she sucked him without hurry. When his fingers clenched in her hair, she took mercy on him and sucked him faster and harder. One hand stroked the length she couldn't fit into her mouth as the other squeezed his balls.

He growled as she brought him closer to the edge.

"Lottie, I'm going to come."

She didn't stop. She continued to suck him harder, going faster, wanting him to lose his control.

"Charlotte," he cried as his balls tightened in her hand and his cock swelled in her mouth.

She swallowed his release, not letting him go until he pulled her hair to pop her off him.

He sank to the floor next to her, pulling her in close. "Did I tell you how perfect you were?"

She smiled, her head resting on his chest as she listened to his erratic heartbeat.

"You mentioned it."

"That was the most beautiful sunset I've ever seen."

"Oh, Goddess, it's not over yet."

She laughed when she noticed his cock beginning to stir. "Already?"

"Always. Now get back up and watch the rest of the sunset as I have my dirty way with you."

Hades had to help Charlotte back into position, her muscles still lax from her orgasm. He assisted her by placing her hands back where they had been before adjusting her exactly where he wanted her. He pushed her legs apart and entered her in one hard thrust.

"Hades," she cried out as he kissed the back of her neck.

Her cry was all he needed to unleash his passion on her. Hades pounded into her. Her arms went weak, and she leaned against the wooden wall as he thrust deeper. His strokes hit a spot deep inside of her at the angle he had her in. Hades grasped her hair and pulled her head back, kissing her deeply as he continued his punishing thrusts.

Charlotte was still sensitive from the last orgasm and sucking him to completion turned her on more than she would have liked to admit. Her orgasm began to form, rushing down the back of her spine, heating her belly.

"You're so wet," he whispered in the back of her neck as he pulled almost all the way out and pushed back in. Charlotte's body quaked as her orgasm took hold of every nerve ending.

"Come with me, Goddess."

Charlotte's head arched as she came, screaming into the night, allowing the darkened sky to swallow her cries. Hades grunted behind her, and his movements became more jerky as he neared his climax.

"Come for me, Pirate."

With a roar, she could feel his release filling her as he pulsed inside of her, prolonging her release.

"That's my Lottie," he told her as he helped her right her clothing.

Charlotte leaned back against Hades' solid chest as they watched the night sky. She began to shiver, the wind more intense so high up.

"Can your legs handle going down, or do you need me to carry you?"

She laughed and leaned her head back on his shoulder. "You can't carry me all the way down."

"I would if you asked it of me."

Charlotte kissed his cheek as she opened the hatch and started down the rungs. She hadn't made it down three rungs before Hades stopped and lurched back up to the crow's nest.

Startled, Charlotte heard him mutter under his breath as he pulled out his spyglass. She held still, the coldness of the rungs seeping into her fingers with no notice.

"Lottie, climb down quickly and move straight to Jackal. Do you hear me?"

She wanted to ask what was happening. She wanted to scream at him she wouldn't be doing any of that until he explained his orders, but she resisted and followed his command. The urgency in Hades’ voice had her on high alert and she wanted to know what he had seen in his spyglass.

Chapter Seventeen

Charlotte hurried down the rungs, grateful when she made it to the deck uninjured. Hades jumped down behind her, missing the last rungs, and placed his hand on her lower back as he guided her toward Jackal. The crew greeted them but held back on anything else when they noticed the intensity on Hades' face.

Jackal's hands were white as he gripped the wheel in one hand and his spyglass in the other.

"Do you see it?" Hades asked in a whisper. "Is it nearing us?"

"I just saw them, Captain. They're headed straight toward us." Jackal shook his head. "I'm going to go monitor from the crow's nest. They'll be on us soon."

"What's happening?" Charlotte asked, already figuring out what Hades was going to say but needing confirmation just the same.

"The Royal Navy is headed our way."

"Navy?" she screeched.

"Not the whole navy, just one of them. And we aren't going to be able to outrun them. Goddess, you're about to be in your first pirate battle."

Charlotte's knees shook and she locked them to keep them still. Her head began to swim as black spots appeared in her vision.

"Breathe, Lottie. I won't let anything happen to you."

Charlotte sucked in the refreshing ocean air, filling her lungs with the frigid air enveloping her. "I'll be fine. I know you'll keep me safe."

Hades stared at her, his jaw clenched as he studied her face. She watched him right back.

"As much as I want to, I'm not going to lock you in our room until this hassle is over."

"Hassle? You're calling a royal navy ship currently headed our way a hassle?"

"Inconvenience?"

"Hades, this isn't something to be taken lightly. Be serious."

"I am serious, Lot. They are headed our way, and we don't have the wind to outrun them. We are going to have to fight them. I want you to watch your back. Persephone will win. She's strong, but this will be bloody, and the carnage will be immense. They are desperate, and we weren't on alert to catch them before they got too close."

"I'll watch my back." She kissed him hard on the mouth. "Thank you."

Hades didn't ask what she was thanking him for. He knew. He knew that not forcing her to hide and allowing her to fight beside the crew was what she would want even if it wasn't what he wanted. She would go crazy if she was stuck below, not knowing what was happening above deck.

"Don't thank me, Lot. This is going to be bloody." His eyes appeared tired as he held her close. "If I didn't know you'd sneak up if I sent you downstairs. I'd lock you in there myself."

Charlotte stopped him with her lips. "I know. I'll be safe. You must promise me you'll be safe too."

"Goddess, I just got you back in my life. I won't do anything to lose you again."

Hades rang the bell next to the wheel, not letting go of Charlotte as he alerted the crew. The crew gathered, and unsettled murmuring flowed around them as they waited for Hades' announcement.

"A Royal Navy ship is headed toward us. The wind isn't strong enough to outrun them. We'll be fighting soon."

The crew threw their hands up, cheering and yelling their imminent victory.

"We'll kill the bastards," someone hollered, causing another cheer to erupt.

"This will not be a normal fight. They are desperate. They know they are losing the war, and they have declared us an enemy as much as the colonies. When you have nothing to lose, you fight as if you don't care about tomorrow."

"We have too much to lose to not care about tomorrow, Captain. We'll fight harder," Pappi shouted, getting the crew into a rowdy mess.

"Man the decks, men. Prepare for battle." At Hades' orders, all celebrating ceased and the crew snapped into order.

Charlotte's mouth dropped open as the efficiency of the crew. They moved in a well-choreographed dance. It was what Charlotte assumed a waltz looked like in a large ballroom she'd never attended. Although she was certain she preferred doing a jig on the deck while a group of rowdy pirates sang a bawdy sea shanty.

"Rest. I'll get you when you need to warm up."

"I can't sleep." She stared at him in shock that he even suggested she attempt to sleep.

"I didn't say sleep. I said rest. You need all your energy for the fight. You need to have all your facilities when they reach us. I'm not letting you get hurt because of some ridiculous misstep that could have been prevented."

"How close are they?"

"I'm turning the ship toward them. It will catch them off guard with not having the time they thought they had to reach us. We will get there soon enough. Now get some rest."

Charlotte pulled out a large woolen blanket and laid it on the deck, refusing to leave him. She tried to relax as she put her arm under her head and stared at the stars. Hades' head blocked her view of the vast sky, but her new view was so much better.

"I'm not leaving." Her arms tensed under her, wondering if he would pick her up and toss her over his shoulder.

"Charlotte," he whispered her name as if he were exasperated but amused as well. He shrugged out of his jacket and laid it on top of her. "Keep warm. You don't want to be sore before the fight starts." He kissed her on the forehead before going back to the wheel.

Charlotte was one with the ship as her back warmed the wood underneath her. She felt the subtle shift of the ship as Hades brought it around. Charlotte's heart was hammering in her chest as she thought of different scenarios this battle would entail.

She snuggled deeper into the blanket, pulling Hades' jacket up to her nose so she could inhale him. Filling her lungs with his scent. She wasn't sure if she was shivering from the cold, or fear that Jackal's prediction was finally coming to fruition.

She went over everything she knew, which she realized wasn't much. A navy ship was approaching. No, a desperate navy ship was approaching them. She forced her breathing to slow like Agatha had taught her when she was assisting her in a dire situation. Charlotte was aware she wasn't the strongest swordsman, and she was about to battle well trained hardened soldiers. She shivered again and this time she knew the reason.

She needed to be smart. She trusted the men on this ship to do what they were supposed to do to keep Persephone afloat. It was her she was worried about. She needed to ensure she wasn't a weakness for them, refusing to put any of them in peril. She would stay and fight, but she would do it with her head on her shoulders.

Charlotte silently vowed she wouldn't put any of these men in danger. She was not going to be a liability to them. The stars weren't keeping her mind off the impending battle as they normally would. Sitting up, she pulled her knees to her chest and placed her chin on them, watching Hades' back as he steered the ship toward what she knew was going to be a bloody battle.

Unbridled anger surged through her when she moved her focus off Hades and toward where they were headed. As she surveyed the calm splendor of the ocean, her anger pulsed through her. The calm was about to burst into a bloody battle where people wouldn't make it to the next dawn, and she hated it. The unjustness of the whole situation frustrated her.

Charlotte thought back to her conversation with Hades when she found out he was the pirate the Royal Navy was in search of. When she asked him why he risked it all for the colonies, his answer was simple.

Freedom.

Freedom was his answer.

Persephone was her first taste of freedom, and these men were going to try to ruin it.

Charlotte jumped up, no longer able to stay still any longer. Hades' hands gripped the wheel as his eyes searched the blackened night. Charlotte couldn't see what he was so intent on, but she hated it nonetheless. Wishing she could see the ship as it neared them but also grateful that she couldn't.

“We’re getting close. They are going to be panicking when we reach them. I guarantee they were not expecting me to turn toward them, and that will have them making mistakes.”

Charlotte wrapped her arms around him, resting her head on his back. She matched his breathing, absorbing the calm he exuded. Quicker than she expected, men started yelling.

It was time.

The excitement was palpable.

Hades began barking orders. Charlotte stepped away, taking the sword Cerberus handed her.

“Thank you, Cerb.” She wanted to beg the boy to go back downstairs where he would be safe, understanding Hades’ need to have her in the same place. She bit her tongue as she realized she had a new focus in this battle.

She was going to make sure Cerb was safe.

Charlotte felt sick as the ship became visible under the full moon. Soon enough, she could see small specks moving around the ship’s deck, and she realized they were people. People who wanted to hurt the man she loved.

The first cannon fire was loud. Louder than she thought was possible. It echoed off the water, causing her ears to ring from the intensity.

The crew held their collective breath as the ball fell short and splashed into the water. With the first shot being fired, it had begun.

The ship flanked Persephone, putting them parallel to each other. Jackal was shouting orders from above as Hades steered the boat and barked orders of his own. The next shot was fired and once again it fell short.

“The bastards can’t reach us, Captain. They are probably short in their pants too.” The pirates laughed hardily, but Charlotte could feel the tension in all of them.

This was only the beginning and she knew it. Soon both ships were volleying cannonballs at each other. Both ships were incrementally getting closer. The first cannon to hit the navy ship made a horrid crashing noise as it catapulted through the side of the ship.

The pirates’ celebratory roar was cut short as the navy ship shot back, and the heavy ball ripped through the upper deck. Charlotte stared in horror as it ricocheted off the deck and lodged itself in a crew member’s chest.

His shocked expression stayed with him as he crumbled to the ground. The first blood went to the navy ship. Smoke littered the air and the stench of gunpowder surrounded Charlotte in a haze of desperation.

She held on to her sword as they neared the navy ship. Hades had a large grin on his face as they sent out ropes, connecting Persephone to the other ship.

Charlotte was in awe as the crew swung onto the other ship. Swords at their hips and daggers in their mouths. The smoke made it cloudy, but the sound of metal meeting metal was unmistakable.

Charlotte noticed some of the navy had got around the crew and were now boarding Persephone. This was her time.

"Be safe." Hades kissed her. Jackal came down and grabbed the wheel as Hades unsheathed his sword. "Keep her steady," he ordered Jackal.

"Stay safe. I'm going over," he ordered Charlotte as he jumped onto the deck. The few men who had made it over to Persephone were dispatched quickly by the pirate crew with efficient deadliness.

Through the smoke, Charlotte watched Hades sail across the air, landing on the deck of the navy ship with a grin on his face. She lost him in the smoke as cannon fire continued to hail across both ships and men engaged in battle.

Screams and victory cries rang out around Charlotte as she moved toward Cerb. Being that not many men were getting across to Persephone, Cerb was safe from battle at the moment.

She wasn't sure how many men were on the ship and how many would make their way over before the night ended, but she needed to ensure Cerb was safe.

She noticed a man sneaking up behind one of the crew as he fought another. Charlotte wrenched her sword and brought it down on his back, not worrying about propriety as blood sprayed across her body. If he wasn't man enough to face his opponent, then she wouldn't feel bad about stabbing him in the back.

"Thank you, Lottie," the pirate said as he turned to see the man fall to the deck.

Chapter Eighteen

More men flooded over to Persephone, most likely to flee from the destruction the pirates were causing on their ship than to fight. Charlotte fought next to Cerb. Her arms burned as she gripped her sword strike after strike.

Sweat and gore covered her face, arms, and everywhere else. The smell of smoke and blood perfumed the air. Charlotte and Cerb were good swordsmen, but the soldiers were excellent, their skill far outmatching hers.

Thankfully, the combination of Cerb and Charlotte matched the soldiers. They fought hard. Charlotte blocked out the sounds around her. If she concentrated on her surroundings, she would lose her focus on ensuring Cerb and the others were safe. She trusted Hades and the crew to get them out of this mess, and she refused to worry.

"Interesting," a deep baritone voice said from behind Charlotte.

She turned her sword at the ready. Her muscles twitched from exertion. Charlotte would have dropped the heavy weapon, but her fingers had cramped around the metal, not allowing the digits to release.

The man in front of her wasn't an ordinary soldier. His uniform was crisp, a royal navy blue in impeccable condition. Not a strand of his blond hair was out of place as his blue eyes feasted on her blood-soaked body.

"My men reported there was a pirate woman on this ship. I had to see for myself, thinking they were battle worn and wishing to see the illusion of a woman on a pirate ship. Imagine my shock."

Charlotte gripped her sword tighter, bringing it above her shoulders, the weight impossible to carry, but refusing to let it go. "Imagine their shock when I'm the one to bring you down," Charlotte sneered, the dried blood cracking at her smile.

"Fascinating," he said. "But that isn't going to happen." In a flash, the captain pulled Cerberus from his back, placing a pistol against his head.

Everything in Charlotte stopped as she stared at the fear pouring off Cerb's face. He may have been a pirate in training, but he was still a fourteen-year-old boy.

"Let him go." Her voice was void of the terror she was feeling. She needed to sound as if she were in control and not the man with the pistol.

"I plan to. In exchange for you."

Charlotte dropped the sword to the deck, the tip plunging into the blood-coated wood. Her hand still held on to the hilt, but the sign of surrender was there.

"Give me your word you'll not harm him."

"No, Lottie, Cap'in will have my head." Cerb realized his mistake as soon as the words left his mouth.

The man holding him now knew she meant something to Hades. A devilish, evil grin split the man's face.

"I thought so." The man threw Cerb to the ground where he slid on the blood-drenched deck.

He motioned for Charlotte with his gun before training it back on Cerb. She dropped the sword, letting it *thunk* on the ground as she moved toward him. With her eyes, she pleaded with Cerb to run and get help as she moved past him.

When she was close enough, he wrenched her to him, pressing the pistol into her temple with enough pressure to have her biting her bottom lip so she wouldn't cry out.

"Do me a favor, Love. Stop holding your cries in. I need to get the crew and the bastard pirate's attention." He jammed the pistol harder into her temple and black spots appeared in her smoke-filled vision.

“I have the woman,” he cried out. More cries echoed out, reverberating across the two boats as the message was made clear.

Hours, months, years, but only seconds and the sound of fighting ceased. A heavy weight landed on the ship. The long, heavy strides eating up the bloody deck could only be one person.

Hades appeared out of the smoke-drenched air. He looked like an avenging apparition. His blood-soaked shirt ripped, his sword held high as if he had all the fortitude to keep ripping the soldiers apart without any fatigue.

“Let her go,” he ordered, his eyes meeting Charlotte’s and traveling down her body to assess what damage had been done to her.

“Not going to happen, Hades.” He rammed the pistol into the side of Charlotte’s head to assert his dominance.

Charlotte would have rolled her eyes at the ridiculous show of male strength if she weren’t in pain.

“You want me, not her.”

Loud thuds continued to litter the deck, letting Charlotte know that Persephone’s crew was coming home to her. Tears stung the back of her throat, but she swallowed them down. She would not cry in front of them. Before the battle, she vowed she wouldn't put them in danger, that she would be an asset to the crew, and here she was, their downfall.

"Actually, I think I want her." His head moved, and she assumed he was surveying the crew just as she had done moments before. "Greetings, pirates. I have a proposition for you."

"State your purpose," Hades growled.

"You are not in charge here."

Charlotte felt the side of her head split where the gun was pushed into it. Blood trickled down her cheek as she stayed locked on Hades. She saw the wrath in his gaze. She wasn't sure when, but she was positive the man who caused her to bleed in front of Hades himself was going to die a horrible death.

She despised the pistol to her head. How weak it made her feel. While training with Hades, she had asked why they practiced with his preferred weapon, the sword. He explained the sword was an honorable weapon, and to use a pistol on the sea was for cowards. Jackal took her aside and explained the gun powder was too unpredictable with the sea mist, and they saved it for the cannons, which did more damage than a pistol ever could.

Except when someone held one to your head in front of the pirate captain, Hades. That pistol had the possibility of damaging many people and at least one person, the one holding the pistol, was going to die.

Charlotte gritted her teeth, refusing to show any emotion while Hades watched. She would not make this harder on him or make him do anything rash.

"This proposition is for your crew."

The hair on the back of Charlotte's head tingled at the swarmy tone of his smug voice. Charlotte resisted the urge to headbutt him. She wanted vengeance and she knew the hellfire in her eyes matched the fire burning in Hades.

"What's your proposition?" Jackal asked, sick of the theatrics the man with the pistol was displaying.

"Ahh, a man of action. Here is my proposition and I'll only say it once, so listen well, you filthy scourge. I'm going to take this disgusting little pirate with me."

The crew protested. They were silenced immediately when he slapped the pistol across Charlotte's face. Her lip split against her teeth and blood streamed down her chin. Charlotte didn't move, but the fire burned throughout her whole body, scorching her insides and metamorphosing her into something different. Something powerful.

She silently vowed she would be the one to end this man's life when it was time.

"I'm going to take her, and you're going to deliver your captain to me in England where I will collect the bounty on his head. I'll even allow you to deliver your cargo to the colonies before turning him in."

"And why would you do that?" Jackal asked, wary of the proposal.

"To get you to do my bidding, of course. The war is over. The colonies are going to win their independence soon. I'm done with this life, and his bounty will allow me a luxurious life. The amount of money you'll receive from the delivery of your cargo, I assume, will allow all of you to do the same. By giving you the money from your cargo, it will ensure you'll do what pirates do best and look out only for yourselves and turn your captain in."

"And what if we don't?" Pappi asked.

Charlotte knew what was going to be said before it was out of his mouth.

"Then I'll turn her in instead. It will be a scandal for the ton. A woman pirate was the one who escaped the Royal Navy for so long, only to be caught by me. Either way, I'll get my money."

"And what will you do with her after they've turned me over and you've collected your bounty?" Hades still watched her, not giving the man with the pistol any attention. All of it on her.

"I'll let her go. Your crew can do with her what they want."

"And she won't be harmed?" Hades asked.

"Stop," she cried, but the pistol smacked her in the side of the head, causing her to bite her tongue. She spat blood on the deck, letting it mingle with all the blood that had been shed in this ridiculous fight.

She knew what Hades was thinking, and she refused to allow him to lose the freedom he so desperately craved because of her. She would beg the man with the pistol to turn her in. She would tell everyone she was the pirate Hades to save the man she loved.

"You have my word. I will turn myself in the moment my ship hits English land. If you promise not to hurt her."

Charlotte let the tears fall, which mingled with the blood still trickling down her face. She wanted to tell him she would sacrifice herself for him. She wanted to tell him how much she loved him, but the man with the pistol did not deserve to witness either confession.

"You have my word. I will not hurt her."

“We will follow your ship then. There is no reason for us to go to the colonies.” Hades’ hands clenched as he realized how helpless he was.

She glanced around the crew, hoping one of them would talk some sense into Hades.

“No, Pirate. You will deliver the cargo you are holding. I do not trust you not to attack on the way back to England’s shores. Are we in agreement?”

Hades’ jaw clenched as he finally moved his gaze from hers and allowed it to land on the man. The man he would watch die soon.

“We have an agreement.”

Charlotte wanted to tell him so many things, but words failed her and she was certain that if she tried to talk, she would get hurt.

“Good.” Then he removed the pistol. “I am an honorable man, Pirate. She will not be harmed unless you do not show up on English shores, and even then, it will not be me hurting her but the royal guard.”

Hades swallowed hard, and Charlotte’s heart was not following her, but staying with Hades on that blood-soaked deck.

“Don’t do anything stupid, Pirate.” He yanked Charlotte by the arm and led her to the ropes where he maneuvered them onto his ship.

Chapter Nineteen

"Captain?" a man with a blood-splattered face watched in confusion as the captain put her down on the bloodied deck.

Charlotte smirked when she realized their deck was covered in blood. Her pirates did well.

"I brought a prisoner, Jenken," he answered, pushing the pistol in her lower back.

"Did you bring the filthy morsel for us, Captain?" one of the disgusting crew members asked, making the rest of the men Hades should have taken down cheer.

"Is this how you treat women aboard your ship, Captain?" she sneered. "Because I will tell you, the pirates you curse treated me better. These are your gentlemen?"

He dug the pistol into her back. She stumbled but caught herself, hiding her smile, knowing she had found a sore spot.

"No one will touch her," he ordered as he jabbed her harder.

"How do you know the whore is a woman? She's dressed as a filthy pirate," one of the men in the small mob cried out.

“Do not question my orders,” he shouted as he moved the pistol to her side and grasped her arm. He propelled her down the steps. Charlotte tripped on the uneven surface. He didn’t stop to let her right herself. He just gripped her arm harder, dragging her the rest of the way.

Charlotte’s shins were bleeding when he finally threw her in a room. Charlotte caught herself before falling on the floor. She would do her best not to show weakness in front of this monster.

“You will not move from this room.” He snarled. His façade of being a gentleman slipped in front of her eyes, and she knew she was right not showing him her weakness.

The man in front of her was hanging on to his sanity by his fingernails. She would have to bide her time, pick him apart bit by bit. She saw the determination on Hades’ face when he took her. He would come for her. All she had to do was survive.

“I wouldn’t want to go up on deck with your disgusting crew. I have no issue staying in here until Hades comes to burn this ship to the bottom of the ocean.”

His hand flew down and connected with her cheek. He was too fast, his insanity making him move at a terrifying speed.

Blood filled her mouth from where her teeth bit into her cheek. She swallowed her blood, wanting nothing more than to spit it in his face but knowing she needed to be smart. She had to survive, and provoking his temper wasn't the way to do it.

She had provided him with a glimpse of his future, and she saw fear pass over his irrational gaze before he connected with her cheek. He knew he was on borrowed time.

"You're a fool. Do you really think they are going to save you? The amount of money they will receive from their cargo is more than enough to keep them from any thoughts of heroism. And if they do decide to come save you, the blasted man they call a captain is going to die. And I'll be rich."

"Turn me in. I won't deny your claims. I will tell them that I am the Pirate Hades."

He stood in front of her, his jaw unhinged before he threw his head back and bellowed with evil laughter. "You stupid wench, you fell in love with him. Is that why you're so adamant he is going to save you? I guarantee, you simple-minded idiot, he hasn't thought about you once when I took you off his ship."

Charlotte allowed her eyes to fill with tears. She even threw in a bottom lip wobble to make it look real. She realized after he had backhanded her, she needed to go about her deceit a different way. "He does love me. He will come for me," she sniffled.

"You don't sound so sure." He tipped his head to the side as he studied her.

She let her first tear fall and his mouth tipped up slightly. "He'll come for me?" She said it as more of a question than a statement.

"No, no, he won't. Be comforted your fragile neck will snap and you will die quickly."

"Can I be comforted that you will get me to England to see my quick death without being harmed?" She still had tears welling up and spilling down her cheeks. She felt the tears cut through the blood that still spattered her face.

His nostrils flared at her insinuation that his crew wasn't the gentlemen they were supposed to be under the crown. She saw the rage when she called out his crew on the deck in front of him. She realized this was also a sore spot she needed to take full advantage of to keep herself safe.

"Yes, you will be safe on my ship. It is the least I can do for the amount of money I'll be receiving at the snap of your neck."

"Thank you...?" She trailed off, wanting the name of the dead man in front of her.

"Captain Hutchings," he answered with a tiny bow.

Charlotte's fingers itched to find the nearest object and bludgeon him over the head with it. "Charlotte." She provided instead.

"Now that the introductions are out of the way, I'm going to get us back to English soil as quickly as possible. Sorry, Charlotte, but your neck will not be safe for long."

"I understand," she replied meekly with her head downcast. "Unless Hades gets to me first."

"Idiot," he muttered before leaving the room.

The door snicked shut before another hiss of metal sounded, letting her know she was officially locked in the room, which was fine by her.

Charlotte surveyed the room, scanning it for any makeshift weapon she could find. It was a small chamber with a small cot taking up most of the area. And nothing else. Charlotte let out a delirious giggle at the sight of the sparse room. The bed was put together where nothing could be broken off of it to make a weapon.

Charlotte giggled until tears streamed down her face. A mixture of bone-tired weariness and fear. She sat down on the bed and silently cried out in surprised pain. The bed had a thin mattress on a plank of wood covered only by a threadbare blanket.

She lay down, her body shutting down from the events of the night. Charlotte's eyes had just closed when the door to her room slammed open, hitting the wall before bouncing back.

She sat up quickly, her body on alert, wishing she had a weapon of some sort. A young boy who reminded her of Cerb but was maybe a few years older, walked into the room, holding a basin with a pitcher.

"Yous are supposed to clean up," he told her with disgust on his face.

"Thank you," she said, hoping to soften the young boy toward her.

"Shut your trap and wash up. I'll be back to collect the water in five minutes, and Captain said if yous break anything to try to fashion a weapon with the shards, he will not guarantee your safety for the remainder of the trip." With his threat delivered, he shut the door and engaged the lock.

Charlotte kneeled on the floor where he had set the water and grabbed the cloth. Charlotte peeled off her blood- and sweat-hardened clothes and felt something hard in her pocket. She pulled out the queen chess piece she had been carrying around for luck.

She squeezed it in her hand until it dug into her palm, a comforting weight although if she had to choose, she would have rather had her letter opener. A wicked smile graced her face. She was going to be fine, and Captain Hutchings' death was going to be bloody. She went to work scrubbing off what she could with vigor. She halved the water in the basin and the pitcher, hoping to keep some of the water clean longer.

The ice-cold water chilled her skin, but she didn't care as she washed what she could. She kept a constant countdown going in her head, not wanting the young boy to walk in on her naked. She hated the thought of putting on her clothes and decided to wrap herself in the thin blanket for a while before having to put on the blood-drenched clothes.

Just as Charlotte was wrapping the blanket around her, the young boy barged into the room again. His eyes went wide at her now clean face. She wasn't sure what his surprise was, but she wondered if seeing her no longer bathed in the blood of his ex-crew members might help her gain an ally.

"Get dressed. Captain says he doesn't want yous dressing like a pirate whore on his ship. He says the reason the men aren't acting like gentlemen is because you're dressed like a whore. Yous dress like a respectable lady, they'll act the way an English gentleman should." He threw a yellow dress at her feet and slammed the door, locking it behind him.

Charlotte stared at the ugly yellow dress, remembering the dress she was wearing when her world opened to what should have been. All of the lonely days, the snide remarks from her aunt, the cruel intentions of her brother, and the loveless relationship with her father were worth it to have Hades in her life.

She had suffered, she had survived, and Hades was her prize for enduring all of it. This she would also endure, and then she was done. She wasn't going to let life make her suffer any longer. She was going to get her happily ever after with Hades and the whole world wouldn't dare attempt to take it away from her again.

All she had to do was survive this final inconvenience, and she would.

And then no more foolishness. She had met her quota and bore it with dignity and grace as was ingrained in her. No longer. She was a strong pirate, but she was an even fiercer woman.

Charlotte pulled the abhorrent dress on with a smile. It resembled her wedding dress; she almost thought it was one and the same. As if the repulsive Captain Hutchings had plucked it off her floor to bring this nightmare to another level of hell.

Charlotte finger combed her hair and plaited it quickly, not knowing how long she would have before the nasty man came back. She lay back down on the torturous bed and put her arm under her head, the queen piece still clutched in her hand as she fell into a light sleep.

"Get up, harlot," the young pirate yelled as the door burst open.

Charlotte was already up, hearing the patter of his clunky feet coming near the door. He stopped and stared as she stood up in the yellow abomination.

"Yous looks like a woman," he said, looking utterly gobsmacked as he continued to stare.

Charlotte opened her mouth to tell him she wasn't a woman, but a pirate, but she thought better of it and snapped her mouth closed. She hadn't given up hope that she'd be able to befriend him.

"What's your name?" she asked instead.

"James. Now quit dallying and follow me." His young face hardened as if he forgot his task for a moment but was back to his assignment.

"Where are we going?" she asked, following behind him.

He didn't answer, but after a couple minutes, she realized he didn't need to answer as she walked into the large dining hall. The noise abruptly stopped when she stepped in behind

James. All the soldiers stared just as James had done when he'd walked in on her.

Charlotte recognized the predatory gleam in some of their eyes and vowed she would steal some form of weaponry before the meal ended.

"Bring her here, James." Captain Hutchings sat at the end of a long table, his uniform crisp as if he hadn't almost been brought down by a pirate ship the night before.

Charlotte wasn't an idiot. She knew they had been winning the fight. He'd been lucky to capture her. If it weren't for her foolish mistake of getting caught, he'd be at the bottom of the sea this very instant.

Charlotte trudged over to him, taking stock of everyone she passed. She spotted injuries, exhaustion, and the worst, lust. She memorized every one of them for when Hades came to claim her.

"You look lovely," the captain stated as he stood, pulling her chair out for her to sit.

Charlotte used the manners her aunt had forced upon her day after day, thanking him and sinking gracefully into the chair.

"My wife will be upset the dresses I bought her are ruined, especially being her favorite color, but with the money your pretty little neck will earn me, I'll be able to provide her all the yellow dresses her perfect heart desires."

Charlotte wanted to gag on the bite of bread she'd just delicately placed in her mouth. She nodded. "I do hope that will be soon, Captain Hutchings. I would hate for Hades to catch up with you and leave your bereft wife without her gowns."

She knew it was a gamble baiting the captain the way she did, but she needed to know how fast the ship went and if she would be saved on sea or on land. Although last night, as she'd fallen asleep, she had come to terms with the fact she would trade her life for Hades without regret.

"So eager to die. I assure you, Charlotte, this ship is the fastest ship in the royal navy. We will be on the English shore soon enough. I suggest enjoying your last few weeks of your life."

I would suggest the same, Charlotte thought as she took another small bite of bread. She wasn't hungry, but she needed to keep up her strength for whatever would come her way.

"I will take your suggestions to heart." Charlotte grabbed the bottle of rum on the table and poured a generous amount in the glass before her.

Before it could reach her mouth, his hand clamped over her wrist in a painful embrace. He took the liquor from her hand and moved it to the other side of him.

"You will act like a lady while on this ship. My men will act as gentlemen to you as long as you act with the grace of a woman. Do you understand me?"

Charlotte nodded while she gritted her back teeth. As much as she loved Hades with her whole heart and soul, she decided in that moment, as he continued to clench her wrist in a punishing hold, she would kill the man bruising her skin but not until Hades came for her. She would not allow him to break her or kill her. Hades would appreciate the sentiment of staying alive and slaying her enemy more than the self-sacrifice of dying for their love by killing him at that moment.

She had planned on killing the man and burning the ship to the bottom of the ocean but also had accepted if the opportunity did not come, she would die for Hades. That was before the bones in her wrist were ground together by the hands of the tyrant next to her.

"I understand you took on heathen ways while on that disgusting ship, but you will not act like that while on this ship," he hissed as he released her wrist, slinging it to the wooden tabletop.

Charlotte didn't have time to stop the momentum, and her wrist and hand slammed hard into the wood, making a loud, painful *thunk* as it hit the table. Charlotte took her hand and laid it on her lap, moving it in different ways to assess the damage. It wasn't broken, but it would be swollen and painful for a while from his treatment.

The rest of the meal went by slowly, and the looks the measly crew was giving her were getting more lascivious. When James was summoned to take her back to her room, Charlotte was relieved. It seemed Captain Hutchings had an easily triggered temper. Charlotte watched as he lashed out at some of his men for acting in what he branded as inappropriate. He screamed at his men when their looks began to linger too long on her and chided her for unladylike behavior.

When James locked her in, Charlotte pulled out the fork she was able to pilfer from the meal, holding it close to her as if it were her salvation.

Charlotte practiced the moves Hades had taught her, brandishing her fork as a dagger. She moved around the small room, not wanting to lose any of the strength she had built while she was on Persephone.

Chapter Twenty

The days blended together and Charlotte feared she would die of inactivity. James would escort her to two meals each day, marking the passage of time. Charlotte cherished the moments she was on the deck, breathing in the sea air. It made her feel closer to Hades, knowing they were inhaling the same briny air.

After a week of being on the navy ship, Charlotte felt as if her skin was too tight for her body. She was bored only having the two events to fill her day. She would practice with her fork every day when she was locked in the small room, the only thing she had that was her own. At night, she would stash her fork under the thin mattress and hold the queen piece as she slept, dreaming of the many ways she could kill Captain Hutchings.

After another week of the same day, James summoned her to the deck in the midmorning. Charlotte glanced at the fork-shaped lump in her mattress as she left the stifling room. She took in huge gulps of air when they made it to the top deck.

As much as she wanted to kill the captain, she realized what a huge mistake it would be. She may be strong, but she wouldn't be able to hold off a whole ship full of soldiers, even though Hades and his crew had greatly diminished them. Not that she didn't dream about it in the late-night moments when sleep wouldn't come visit her.

"Charlotte." He bowed in front of her, and she had to stop her lip from twitching from the pure hate she felt for the man in front of her.

"Captain." She wanted to ask why she was out of her prison, but she didn't want to poke his temper if he was going to allow her more exercise.

"My men and I have been discussing how arduous this journey has been."

She kept her mouth shut, not able to figure out what he had brought her up there for. Normally, she was able to read him, but she was baffled at his reasons for bringing her on deck, so she stayed quiet.

"I thought it would be a treat for you to entertain my men tonight after dinner." The gleam in his eyes was purely malicious.

Charlotte's anger rose and she wished she hadn't left her fork back in the small room. "Entertain?" She said the word in a question form.

He frowned, grasping her upper arm and steering her over to the railing of the ship. She had the fleeting thought he might throw her overboard, and she almost wished he would, wondering if she could float until Hades found her.

He squeezed her arm, which was his favorite form of punishment. Since she had been on the ship, anytime she displeased him in any way, he would grasp her arm in a punishing grip and squeeze until it was obvious he would leave a mark.

Charlotte counted every one of the bruises he left on her body. He would bear the mark of each one he left on her before she took his life in the most brutal way her imagination could conjure.

"Why do you keep disrespecting my men?" he hissed.

"I wasn't, Captain. I was just asking what entertainment I would be providing for your men?" She made her voice as docile as she could with her back teeth ground together. Every day, she hated this man even more and she couldn't wait until she could end his life.

"Don't act innocent. Your disgusting brain was thinking of the way you entertained those filthy pirates on the ship." His hand squeezed harder and Charlotte almost screamed out.

Almost.

"You will be entertaining as a true lady would. The least I can do is send you off to your death without any lurid acts tainting the last days of your life."

"I have no skill as a true lady," she said, the bile in her throat rising as he continued to squeeze. She thought of the sea shanties she'd learned on the Persephone and wondered how many bruises she would receive if she sang one of those.

"You will think of one by the end of the night. After your performance, I will read from the Bible as you seem to need to be reminded of the power of God. I might even be able to save you before you die."

"Thank you for your thoughtfulness. I'm sure I will think of something to do before nightfall."

"That's better." He gave one more squeeze before tucking her arm into his and escorting her down to the room. She wanted to scream when the lock clicked into place, but she had nothing to muffle the sound as the threadbare blanket and thin mattress were no match for the wrath she wanted to vent.

Charlotte paced the small room, begging Hades to hurry. She would survive all the way to England if she had to, but she didn't want to. She wanted to feel the hot spray of the captain's blood on her face as she drove her sword, fork, hands into his heart and watched the final beat with her own eyes.

Charlotte grinned as she thought of what she would do to entertain the so-called gentlemen on board.

The captain was practically giddy as the food was placed in front of them. Charlotte was also giddy, but for a very different reason.

"And what will you be entertaining us with tonight?" he asked as he popped a piece of bread in his mouth.

"I decided to grace you with a song," she replied in a sickly-sweet tone her aunt had pounded into her.

"A song. Yes, a song will do."

Once again, Charlotte had the rebellious thought of singing one of the sea shanties, but that was for her imagination only. Maybe she would sing one as she hacked into his body as she killed him.

"Gentlemen." Hutchings got up from the table and addressed the men in the dining hall. "Lady Charlotte had graciously decided to sing a song for us tonight. She will get to act like a true lady before she dies at the hands of the English for her treason."

"Or I'll be able to live into my old age if Hades is turned in. Isn't that the bargain you made?"

"Oh, you simple-minded female. Those pirates are not going to turn in their captain for you. They will take their money and retire, or they will continue to run against the law, and I will find them on a different day and kill them then. You will not be saved."

Charlotte bit the inside of her lip to keep from telling him the only reason he was alive at the moment was because he had captured her. His ship was losing that momentous battle, and he got lucky finding her out of all the pirates on the ship.

When the meal had been cleared away, the captain led everyone outside in the crisp, chilly air. Charlotte stood on the raised deck and began to sing. She chose the song with care, and she sang it with all the hatred and frustration she felt.

She sang a song she had heard in a bar one night when she helped Agatha stitch up the barkeep. It was a song of vengeance from a man whose love was stolen away by an evil neighbor. She sang with all the passion she could conjure as she avoided the captain's eyes, not sure if he would be happy with her choice.

When the song ended in a haunting melody of the two finding each other after the neighbor had been killed, the ship was silent. The sounds of the ocean smacking the side of the boat as the mast snapped in the wind were the only things she could hear.

She got up the courage to lift her head, but before she could connect with the captain, the crew cheered uproariously. She took a small bow as a hand she was used to fastened around her in a pressure she was also familiar with.

"Stupid, you are lucky my men are so starved for entertainment they weren't offended. I suggest you pick another song to sing tomorrow."

"Yes, Captain," she replied, barely holding her smile at bay.

He gave her one final squeeze before sitting down on a chair one of his men had carried out for him. Under the light of a lamp, he began reading from his Bible. Charlotte didn't listen to the drivel coming out of the horrid man. She refused to listen to anything that came out of his mouth, especially as he handpicked the vilest stories he could find of vengeance and jealousy.

As he continued to preach, Charlotte thought of the next song she would sing for tomorrow. She could be more subtle in her message if she had time to think about it. She knew the choice of the song for that night was dangerous, but the rebel pirate in her needed to stretch some. The only time the pirate singing in her veins was able to make its appearance was when she was thrusting her fork in the small room.

When she was dismissed, James brought her down to the room and locked the door. Charlotte tried to keep her spirits high. It was the most time she had been able to spend out of her room, and she reminded herself she needed to be happy for small things until Hades came for her.

Several weeks later, Charlotte was barely hanging onto her spirit. She wanted to hurt something. Actually, she wanted to hurt someone. Captain Hutchings had become more violent as the days droned on.

She realized he was getting anxious the closer they got to English soil. She wasn't sure if it was fear that Hades would, in fact, catch up with him, or if he was afraid the crown wouldn't accept her as the hunted pirate Hades.

He lost his temper more often and Charlotte had bruises all over her arms and some on her legs where he had pushed her down. She hated she had to be submissive as she waited for Hades to help her kill the entire crew.

Charlotte was in the small prison they called a room, practicing when she heard a sharp inhale. She turned to see James staring at her with awe on his face.

"What are you doing?" he asked, but his voice wasn't accusatory. It was more curious.

Charlotte quickly pocketed the fork, letting it settle next to the queen piece. She hoped he hadn't seen the silver utensil.

"I wasn't doing anything," she replied. In the weeks they had been to sea, she hadn't been able to get James to befriend her. She didn't trust him and was afraid they would shackle her in the brig if he told the captain.

"You were practicing sword fighting," he whispered as he closed the door.

Charlotte braced herself, wondering how far the good captain would go in his punishment.

"Will you teach me?" he asked, shocking them both.

Charlotte eyed him warily, wondering if he was setting a trap for her. She knew they were getting close to English soil, and she needed to be in the best condition she could be when she killed the captain. She had even gone so far as to start singing songs she knew he would approve of. The captain waxed on, that the Bible he had been reading was finally making an impression, as if he were her savior.

He could think he was her savior as much as he liked. For she would be his demise.

"Are you going to tell the captain?" she asked.

"Not if you teach me. I've been begging them to teach me how to sword fight, but they tell me I'm not a gentleman."

James' lip quivered, and Charlotte thought back to the interactions she had witnessed involving James and the crew.

"And why aren't you a gentleman?" Charlotte assumed she knew the answer, but she wanted to make sure before she began pulling the young boy to her side.

"I was born a bastard. They caught me stealing and were going to chop me hand off. The judge sent me to work on the naval ship instead." James rubbed his hand, and Charlotte had a sinking suspicion he didn't even realize he was doing it.

"They can go to the devil. You have been nothing but a gentleman to me." It was a lie, and they both knew it. "I'll teach you, but you cannot let the captain know. You have to promise me, as a gentleman." Charlotte stared at him, wanting him to see the severity of what he was asking her.

If the captain found out she'd been teaching James, who she now surmised he did not respect because of his upbringing, not only would he be punished but her bruise count would go up infinitesimally.

"I promise," he said solemnly and Charlotte trusted him.

It may have been a stupid mistake, but she had been isolated on the blasted ship with no one, and she was lonely. She also figured it wouldn't be a bad thing to have James on her side when it was time to fight. And teaching him how to fight would be a plus.

"Are all of your chores done?" she asked, glancing at the door, afraid the captain would burst in at any moment.

"Not yet. I was delivering this to you." He handed her a freshly laundered yellow dress and Charlotte grimaced at the sight of the offending dress.

"Go finish your chores."

James hurried to leave the room, but she cautioned him. "Do not finish them quickly. Do not look too eager either. If any of the crew gets suspicious, the captain will find out, and we will both be punished."

James nodded at her with more understanding than a young boy his age should. He slowed his pace as he headed for the door. Charlotte smiled as she washed in the water she had left and pulled on the ugly dress.

James was a quick learner. Although it was hard teaching him in such a cramped space, they made do. She never revealed her fork to him, afraid that if he was questioned, he would not be able to keep their secret.

James smiled as he thrust and parried, but as soon as he walked out of the room, he went back to shooting her disgusted glares. If the kid didn't make it as a sailor, he would be a phenomenal actor.

Teaching James had made the two weeks of the arduous journey go by faster. They had become friends, and he shared his stories of when he was on the streets. Charlotte's heart ached at listening to what he had to endure at such a young age.

Charlotte told him of her time on the pirate ship. At first, he didn't believe her, unable to comprehend a band of pirates treated her better than the highest officials of the English Navy. She hoped by the time Hades came, she would have him fully convinced to come with her on the Persephone.

Chapter Twenty-One

A weird aura had fallen over the dining hall. The cutlery scraped against the plates and Charlotte's nerves. She watched the crew, noticing not all of them were unaffected by the grating sounds.

Men's jaws were clenched, and their shoulders were hunched around their plates in a protective gesture. Even Captain Hutchings was more subdued than normal. When dinner had finally cleared away and the horrid sound of scraping silverware was removed, Charlotte's nerves didn't calm.

When she walked outside, she stopped short. The ship was dark. Pitch dark.

The flickering of surrounding lanterns did nothing to clear the blackness away. Charlotte glanced up and noticed there was no moon hanging in the sky.

Sailors glanced toward the sky and quickly away, muttering things she couldn't quite catch before the wind whipped it away. She heard bits of what they were saying. The most captured phrase was *the devil's sky*.

The cool breeze whipped at Charlotte and the hair on the back of her neck came to attention. There was definitely something in the air that had everyone on the edge of losing their minds.

Charlotte wouldn't have been surprised if a fight broke out on the ship tonight, or multiple brawls.

She took the makeshift stage the captain had been making her sing on with shaky legs. The feeling that something was upon them didn't leave her as she prepared to sing. The crew lit extra lanterns to light her up, but the night swallowed the small amount of light they emitted.

The eerie flicker of the flame danced a few inches ahead of the glass before disappearing into the inky blackness. Charlotte began singing. Her voice registered lower as if it too couldn't penetrate the oppressive darkness.

Charlotte sang four songs before the captain dismissed her. She sat on the small stool in the back of the crowd, hoping she could sneak away when he got into his religious rant.

The captain had to have extra lanterns lit for him to see the small text of the Bible he held. The flickering lights encircled him, giving off an evil glow, which Charlotte felt was fitting for the vile man.

The captain must have been bored the other night because his quotes were handpicked about evil women and how they needed to obey the man in their life. Charlotte rolled her eyes as he droned on and on. He glanced up and caught her eyes. Thankfully, it had been in between eye rolls, but she realized she would not be sneaking away until he felt she was fully chastised and he put his Bible away.

The captain continued his rant as she felt her muscles go slack with exhaustion. She hadn't slept well since she had been captured. Even with her extra activity teaching James how to sword fight, her body would not allow her to go into a deep sleep.

Her eyes burned as she fought to keep them open.

Mercy was served when the captain finished his tirade about the wickedness of women and finally shut his Bible. Charlotte stood and pressed her fists into her lower back, stretching out the muscles. The captain had gone on longer than his usual rants and she was ready to go to the room she was held prisoner in.

She would rest until James sneaked into her room for his nightly training. Charlotte moved slowly as the crew went on to their duties, and she was shuffled back to the room with James as her prison guard.

Charlotte and James did not speak to each other on the way down to the room. They were both too afraid to be seen as getting friendly. She feared what the captain would do if he caught James fraternizing with the pirate whore as he was so apt to call her when the rest of the crew wasn't around.

When the captain was around his crew, he would act as if he were the upstanding gentleman he presented to everyone who didn't know him. He called her Charlotte and insisted she act like a lady, hoping it would help her get into the gates of heaven, or at least that was what he would proclaim whenever his crew overheard him. When no one was around, he would grab her tightly and punish her as no gentleman would ever act.

James pushed her into the room with little pressure. She made herself stumble as if he had pushed her harder than he had. She would need to speak with him tonight about making sure he didn't pull his strength because they were becoming friends. She didn't think anyone was watching her interactions with the boy, but one could never be too sure.

He slammed and locked the door, calling her a dirty pirate whore as he left. She knew then he figured out his mistake and was righting the wrong. Charlotte would need to explain to him again that it was okay to be rough with her as long as it made them both safe.

Charlotte lay on the hard bed as she waited for the young boy to come back. The windowless room was darker than normal as well. It was as if the night had crept under the crack in the door and coated the room in its darkness.

Charlotte lowered the lantern's flame, wanting to save the oil for when James arrived. Sometimes he would bring an extra lantern, but there were times when that was impossible. Charlotte nodded off, her body still on edge with the ominous energy blanketing the ship.

James snuck into her room later than normal. He shut the door quietly as if he too felt the portentous atmosphere.

"Did anyone see you?" she whispered to the boy, afraid to even use her voice as if it would summon the captain.

"No," he answered just as quietly. "The crew is muttering something fierce about the devil night. It was easy to sneak down here as nobody was paying any attention. They are all looking upward, begging the moon to return. The captain even lowered the mast so as not to sail too fast, afraid the moonless night will veer us off course. Everyone is being extra cautious, and I guess their mood got to me and made me cautious as well."

Charlotte nodded, understanding the boy's apprehension as she felt it as well.

They sat in silence in the dim room, neither of them getting up for their lesson. After some time, they both stood and began slowly moving to stretch their muscles. Charlotte wasn't even aware that they were both waiting to see if they were going to get caught.

They were both quiet as they went through the motions of a sword fight. Neither of them was trying very hard. Other nights, they had epic battles, each of them scoring points on each other that would have been deadly if they had weapons.

Tonight, they were moving with no real dedication, but neither of them wanted to end the session. Charlotte didn't want to be alone, and she had a feeling James felt the same way.

They were both sweating when the door slammed open. The hinges on the top of the door pulled out of the wooden frame, making it list precariously against the wall.

"I knew something was happening. You were being too docile." The captain pointed at her and Charlotte knew it was her mistake alone that was going to get them both punished.

She glanced at James, but his eyes were locked on the captain's.

"It was my fault. Don't blame the boy." Charlotte stepped in front of James, hoping to protect him from the majority of the punishment.

"You're a pirate witch," he seethed as he stepped into the room.

James moved to her side, and she attempted to push him back, but he refused to hide behind her. "Captain, I was—"

Before James could finish his sentence, Captain Hutchings backhanded him hard enough to send him flying into the wall. Charlotte gasped as she stood in between the Captain and James.

"I should have known a filthy street urchin would befriend the pirate whore," he roared as he glared at the boy getting to his feet. "We gave you everything and you betrayed us. I will see you at the gallows next to her. What were you two doing in here? Conspiring against me?"

"Stop, let him go. I will accept his punishment. It was my idea to teach him."

"You seem to enjoy taking other people's punishments. Do you enjoy pain, Pirate?" He stepped toward her and grasped her wrist, grinding the bones together.

Charlotte stood, refusing to allow her knees to give out as much as she wanted to.

"What were you teaching him?" he asked, crushing her wrist harder.

"I was teaching him basic—"

“Reading,” James cut her off and she was glad for it.

Her brain was having a hard time thinking as he continued to squeeze her wrist.

“Reading? What would filth like you need to read for?” The captain’s sneer was condescending and Charlotte wanted to wipe it off his smug face.

“I wanted to read the Bible,” James answered and Charlotte was impressed at the young boy’s bravado.

He kept a cool head, and Charlotte wondered if he had preemptively thought of the answers in case this happened.

“The Bible.” That moved some of the condescension off his face. He was constantly telling the crew they needed to study the Bible more, and here young James was doing just that.

“You still went against my orders.”

He pushed Charlotte, letting go of her wrist. She righted herself before she fell to the floor and she knew that was the wrong move. He took a menacing step toward her and pushed her until she fell to the ground where he towered over her.

“I told him I would teach him after everyone went to bed and his chores were done. I didn’t want to take him away from your orders.” Charlotte attempted to look contrite, but her wrist throbbed and she was close to being done placating this man.

"You should have told me." He kicked her tender wrist, making her fall further to the ground. "You do not do anything on my ship without my consent." He kicked her again and she felt a rib crack under the toe of his boot.

Charlotte still refused to cry out, which made him angry. She knew he wanted her to submit to him, but on that, she could not pretend.

He kicked her again as he stared at her with his malicious blue eyes. Eyes that should have been beautiful on the muscular man, but they held nothing but hate in them.

"I wanted to make the last few weeks you had left to live pleasant. I gave you my wife's dresses, I fed you at my table, and I allowed you to entertain my men as a woman of your station is meant for. And what do you do? You betray me."

Charlotte stared at him. Her breath was coming in pants. As much as she wanted to appear calm, the pain was leaking out of cracks in the wall she had placed around her heart to hide her emotions.

"You will stay here in this room until we reach English shores. I will call the constable as soon as we dock and request your neck to be snapped by sundown."

"What about your promise to wait for the pirates to turn in Hades?" she asked, her voice higher as it hurt too much to suck in a breath with her rib.

"You stupid woman. They are not going to come for you and as soon as your dirty neck is snapped, I will hunt down and kill every one of them, take the money they bargained your life away for and retire in a life of luxury with my wife."

"I'm going to kill you, and I promise I will not be lenient. Hades will save me."

He had lost his control. Charlotte saw the crazed look in his eyes and knew there was no reason to pretend to be the dutiful prisoner.

"Be careful. You may not make it to English soil if you keep speaking like that."

She spat at him. It landed on his trousers.

He let out a roar, pulling her up by her hair and punching her on the side of the head. Charlotte's ears rang, but she heard another smaller roar. James jumped on the captain's back and began pummeling him with his fist.

Charlotte had forgotten the young boy was in the room. She had been so focused on the hate spewing out of the captain's mouth and her mirroring his filled look with one of her own.

"James, no." She attempted to get out of the captain's grasp as he grappled with James.

James sank his nimble finger into the captain's eye. He screamed, letting go of Charlotte as he snapped James' wrist with a sickening crack.

James crumpled to the ground, staring at his mangled wrist. Charlotte didn't wait. She pulled the fork from its hiding place under the mattress and stabbed the captain in the eye James had tried to poke out.

He screamed a guttural, inhuman sound, grasping for her with flailing arms. Charlotte moved to get away, but he grabbed the skirt of her dress and began hauling her back. Charlotte kicked her heel, landing in the captain's nose. The soft slippers she wore weren't enough to break his nose, but it had enough force to get away.

A loud crash sounded on the upper deck. All three stopped in unison, listening to the commotion above them. For a moment, everything was quiet. Charlotte wondered briefly if she had imagined the loud crash, but it happened again.

A fierce repercussion of numerous cannons happened at once before the ship rocked as the cannonballs hit their mark.

"It appears your day of reckoning has come, Captain."

Bells rang above them. A chorus of screams littered the quiet in between the next cannon volley.

“I suggest you get up there.” Charlotte quirked an eyebrow as the captain glared at her with his one good eye. The other was mangled beyond repair and blood poured down his face as he moved.

He turned to go upstairs, but before he did, he surprised Charlotte by turning around unexpectedly and punching her in the side of the head. Charlotte’s grin went slack as she fell to the floor, blackness taking over her.

A light tapping landed on Charlotte’s cheek. She tried to bat it away, but her hand felt heavy and when she moved it, searing pain shot up her arm.

“Charlotte, you have to wake up.” More tapping on her face.

She was slowly pulled into reality as she realized the fearful voice was James, and there was screaming and a cacophony of noise above her. Charlotte opened her eyes and was grateful for the dim lighting.

“It seems your pirates have come to rescue you.” James smiled, blood crusting the side of his head where Captain Hutchings had connected his fist.

Memories of what had occurred before the captain had knocked her out came back to her in waves. She leaned over and retched, not caring that she was vomiting all over the captain's floor.

"How long was I out?" she asked, her voice harsh from the vomit.

"I don't know, but it seems the pirates have landed. I heard them hitting the top deck and more screams than I've ever heard."

Charlotte and James smiled at each other, reveling in the carnage the pirates were meting out.

"I tried to get the door open, but I can't do it with one hand." James let out a disgusted breath, frustration evident on his young face.

"We'll get out together," Charlotte said as she tried to pat down her hair. She knew she looked a fright, but she hoped she at least looked fierce. She wanted Hades to know she never lost faith in him, and she did all she could to survive until he found her.

Together, Charlotte and James were able to maneuver the broken door enough that they could slip out. When the captain had barged in and caught them, he had mangled the door where the lock wasn't strong enough to hold them in.

Charlotte stood quickly once she had shimmied out into the hall, then held on to James with her good hand as she waited for her world to right itself. She hated that she was down here as they fought. She wanted to be next to Hades, doling out the punishments.

As if conjured from her thoughts, Hades appeared at the top of the landing they were cresting. He looked like an avenging angel, covered in soot and blood. His shirt was torn, but he didn’t appear injured.

Chapter Twenty-Two

His eyes wandered all over her body, assessing her for injuries or mistreatment just as she had been doing to him. His lip curled up as he got to her dress.

"Why is it that every time I rescue you, you are dressed in that godawful color?"

Charlotte laughed and hiccupped into a cry as she blinked away the tears, wanting to listen to his voice for the rest of her life and beyond.

He was beautiful, perfect, and hers. Charlotte rushed to him. She wrapped her arms around him, not caring about her broken rib or her bruised wrist.

"What took you so long?" she scolded, not letting him go as she peppered kisses all over his face.

"Sorry, Goddess, I had to get some things done before I was able to come get you." He held her just as tight as she held him. The sound of his deep baritone voice had tears rushing down her cheeks and onto his shirt.

"Are they all dead?" she asked, not letting him go.

"Not all of them. I saved the captain for you. I didn't think you would forgive me if I took that honor away from you."

"The fight's over?" James said, startling Charlotte.

It was the second time she had forgotten the boy was there.

"Sorry, lad, I didn't see you there. The fight's not over yet, but it will be soon. You can come up and watch my beautiful pirate queen dispatch the captain as the rest of my crew finishes with the last of the scourge."

Hades shifted Charlotte to his side. She refused to unlock her arms or legs from him. Instead, she moved over so Hades could see James fully.

"Hades, this is James. He was the one who kept me sane as I waited for your long-awaited arrival. I've been teaching him how to sword fight, and I think he would make an excellent pirate aboard Persephone."

Hades stuck out his hand for James to shake. James hesitated and she remembered his broken wrist.

"The illustrious captain broke his wrist," Charlotte explained.

Hades' jaw clenched as he then assessed the young boy.

"I'm the one who poked out his eye. Although Charlotte was the one who stabbed it with a fork." James puffed out his chest and Charlotte loved him for his bravery.

"Stabbed him with a fork, you say? I cannot wait to hear this story when we get aboard Persephone, and I'll tell you about her letter opener. I owe you a great debt, James. You looked after my heart, my soul, my life when I wasn't able to and I would be honored if you joined my crew."

Charlotte blinked back tears as James' mouth hung open at the pirate's words.

"It would be my honor," James replied.

"Let's go finish this nonsense so we can get away from this filth," Hades said as he carried Charlotte. James trotted behind them with a huge grin on his face.

Before they reached the deck where the fighting was centralized, Charlotte stopped Hades.

"Put me down."

His gaze roamed over her as he frowned at her request.

"I refuse to look weak in front of that man," she answered his silent question.

"As you wish, Goddess. But I can promise that you could never appear weak to anyone. You are the strongest woman I have ever met."

Charlotte kissed him lightly on the lips, knowing that if she kissed him deeply, she wouldn't stop and James was still dutifully following behind them.

Charlotte walked onto the deck. All she could see was beautiful destruction. The moon still had not appeared, but lanterns lit the deck and fires burned, crackling as they devoured the broken wood.

Skirmishes were happening around the ship, but it appeared the fight was almost over. Charlotte's heart sank as she realized she wouldn't be doling out the punishment she'd been planning for weeks.

Charlotte stepped over the carnage of dead bodies and pieces of the broken ship. Near the helm, Charlotte saw the most beautiful sight. Captain Hutchings was fighting with Jackal, his sword wobbly as if he were straining to hold it, while Jackal's sword was as steady as they came.

Charlotte yelled across the clashing swords and crackling fire. "He's mine, Jackal."

Captain Hutchings glared at her with his one good eye as she made her way toward them. Her smile grew the closer she got to the man who had attempted to break her while she was on his godforsaken ship.

Cerb, who had just smashed a navy crew's face and thrown him overboard, smiled at her, and she could tell the young boy wanted to run to her and hug her, but he held steady.

"It's good to see you, Lottie," Jackal said as he pushed his sword into the captain's back, making him cry out.

"Good to see you both," she said, her voice rough from the emotions she had to push down.

She still refused to allow this man to see any emotion.

"I need a sword. I don't think my fork will do, although it did some considerable damage."

Hades handed her his sword with a small bow. It reminded her of the first time he handed her his sword when she had fought Shark. He trusted her then to take care of herself, and he trusted her now to do the same.

Freedom, she thought wistfully as she grasped the sword hilt.

"I'm not going to fight you, pirate whore." Captain Hutchings spat the word whore, and she felt Hades tense next to her.

"If you best me, I will let you go. There is a rowboat I'll let you escape from." Charlotte held up her sword, waiting for the captain to raise his.

"I refuse to take the word of a pirate."

"Your loss." Charlotte nicked him with her sword, causing his bicep to swell with blood.

He didn't move. He just watched her. She did it again on his other arm, and that did it.

He cried out and put his sword in a fighting position. The metal rang out as they clashed. Fire snapped and popped as the ship continued to burn, but Charlotte ignored all of it. She ignored the fact that Hades was near her for the first time in weeks. She ignored the fact that her home was a rope swing away, and she would be where she belonged with the love of her life.

Charlotte was shocked by how well the captain fought. Especially with one eye. Her wrist was weak and the stabbing pain in her ribs every time the swords met took her breath away. Her rib complained as she sucked in air and her wrist throbbed.

Even though she had practiced almost every night, she had lost some of her muscle. Sweat poured down her face as she fought. The captain's face was lost in anger. She didn't even think he was aware of anything but the need to kill her.

He was pushing Charlotte down the stairs away from the helm. She was on the defense. He was stronger than her and her wrist wasn't going to hold on to the sword much longer. It throbbed with every heartbeat and her forearm cramped as she forced it to hang on.

She knew if she started to lose, even with her promise to let him go, Hades wouldn't allow it and she hated that he would have the pleasure of ending his life.

That thought had a wave of energy surging through Charlotte. She couldn't beat him in strength and in skill, so she needed to be smart.

She noticed a part of the deck that a cannonball had destroyed. He was so focused on Charlotte, she allowed him to push her back, but he didn't notice she was slowly making her way over to the broken part of the ship.

Charlotte knew this was her last chance to kill him before Hades stepped in. Even though she couldn't see him, she could feel his impatience, and honestly, she had been away from him for too long to prolong their reunion.

Charlotte made her move, hoping she had enough strength to pull off her plan. She stepped on one of the broken boards and it lifted, slamming in between the captain's legs. He screamed as she thrust her sword into his stomach. He fell back, a piece of the broken board impaling him through the leg.

His face was still enveloped in hate, and she wasn't sure he even realized he had lost. His sword dropped from his hand as she twisted her sword into his stomach. Charlotte left her sword in him and wrapped her hands around his throat.

She squeezed with everything she had. She brought forth every time he had grasped her arm, but as much as she squeezed, she wasn't strong enough to end him the way she wanted.

Strong hands enveloped hers and Charlotte breathed out a sigh of relief. Hades had come to assist her. Not to take away her vengeance but to help her enact it.

Together, they squeezed and the captain's one good eye bulged. She stared into it until the hatred dulled and his life seeped out of him.

"He's dead, Lot," Hades said in her ear as she still held on to his neck.

His pulse no longer thrummed under her palm. Charlotte released his neck one finger at a time until she sagged against Hades.

"Are you ready to get out of here?" he asked in her ear, not letting her go.

She nodded, and that was all he needed. He pulled out his sword from the captain's belly, wiped it on the dead man's shirt, and sheathed it before pulling her toward him. He ripped a piece of the bloody shirt off the captain and stuffed it in his trousers.

“Burn it down,” he ordered as he grasped a rope and swung them over to the Persephone. Charlotte heard the others land on the deck as well, and she smiled when she saw Cerb and James talking excitedly.

The crew cheered. Hades held up her hand as the navy ship burned behind them.

“All hail my pirate queen,” Hades announced and the cheer was deafening.

He grabbed her and pulled her ear to his mouth. “Marry me, Charlotte. Be my pirate queen from now to eternity.”

“I can’t do that,” she answered. “I’ve been yours since the day I met you. Not since now, but forever.”

He kissed her hard. When he pulled away, he took out the piece of bloody shirt he had torn from the captain’s shirt. He wrapped the bloody cloth around their wrists, binding them together.

Charlotte stared at the beautiful, macabre sight and smiled. Hades winked at her as Jackal sauntered over and performed the fastest wedding ceremony. Charlotte wouldn’t have wanted it any other way.

As the ship of her enemy burned into the ocean, Charlotte bound herself to the only man she’d ever loved. Her dirty, perfect pirate.

After the ceremony, Cook bound Charlotte's wrist and rubbed a salve she had taught him to make on her ribs. He also splinted James' wrist before the boy ran off with Cerb to practice sword fighting.

Cook sent her to bed, telling her he could mend the crew as he had been doing it long before she ever stepped on the ship.

Hades led her down to the room where the chessboard waited for her. The missing queen was still in her pocket. She took it out but couldn't seem to place it back on the board.

"She kept me safe," Charlotte admitted sheepishly.

Hades took the piece from her hand and kissed it. "Then she shall stay with you. Anything to keep you safe."

They made love until the sun shone in through the window and both of them succumbed to exhaustion.

Charlotte slept in Hades' arms, letting herself settle into a deep sleep, knowing she was safe. She was home.

Epilogue

Three years later

Hades

Charlotte is the most beautiful woman, Hades thought as he watched her dry heave into the basin, which seemed have become a permanent fixture next to the bed the past four days.

"Pet, in all the years we've been out to sea, I've never seen you seasick. This is worse than when you imbibed on rum for the first time." He hovered over her. His worry etched on his face so deeply his forehead ached.

"I'm changing course and heading back to the port we'd just left." Hades wiped the sweat brought to him by fear off his face. Seeing the only woman he had ever loved retch for days on end made his soul want to scream with terror.

He watched with bated breath as she wiped her mouth after washing it out with water. She smiled, and if it weren't for the paleness blanketing her face, he would almost believe she was herself.

Hades' heart hammered in his chest as he pulled her into him. The place he would keep her forever. Sickness would not take her from him, he vowed in his head.

"It's not me who's sick, husband." She pulled away and laid her hand on her stomach. Hades looked at her in confusion until he looked down at her carefully placed hand.

His heart stuttered, and his soul rejoiced. Now it was him who felt sick. His wife. His beautiful Goddess was giving him a child. He didn't deserve her, but he was a selfish pirate and he was never letting her go.

His knees hit the floor as he lifted her hand and placed his forehead on her stomach. "A child," he whispered to her stomach in reverence.

She pulled his hair so he would look up at her. "We're having a little pirate."

Hades jumped up and swung her around before placing her down quickly. "Did I hurt you?" His hands fluttered over her as if he didn't know where to touch her.

"You should know I'm sturdier than that."

"That you are, my pirate queen. What do you think about Agatha delivering our baby?"

Charlotte's mouth hung open as she stared at her husband. Hades had confided in her that he moved Agatha to an estate he had won a long time ago the night before her wedding. Agatha had been living happily in a little cottage on his estate, taking care of all the residents.

"What are you suggesting, Hades?" his perfect pirate queen asked, her hands still clutching him.

After she had killed Captain Hutchings, they had been traveling the world. Wherever his pirate queen asked to go, he took her. Money never being an issue.

Hades had taken the last shipment to the colonies when Captain Hutchings had taken her. The crew then used some of the money to paint the ship black, making it almost impossible to detect, especially on a moonless night like the night he launched his rescue.

Those weeks he was apart from Charlotte were the hardest he'd ever endured. The crew avoided him, afraid they wouldn't survive a conversation with their heads still attached. He doubted his choice to go to the colonies every minute they were apart.

Hades knew it was the smart move, but it was unbearable. The only thing that got him through those nights alone without his goddess by his side was his unwavering faith in her strength. It didn't make it any easier, but it was the only thing that kept him holding on.

Most of the crew stayed on, refusing to leave until she had been rescued. Pride filled Hades every time he thought of how dedicated his crew was to his wife and her safety. After the rescue, some of the crew left to find a queen of their own, some found another pirate ship craving the adventure, and the rest sailed on with Hades and Charlotte, making the ship a family neither of them had before.

Charlotte and Hades sailed around the world with their inherited family. Cerb and James were at the helm most of the time now. The little pirates loved the responsibility under Jackal's watchful eye.

"I'm saying I've been Hades for some time now. Maybe I want to be Jack for a while." Hades watched in astonishment as Charlotte realized what he'd just said.

Charlotte leapt into his arms, kissing him deeply, making him groan at her intensity.

"I think I would like that very much, Pirate," she confessed to him. "As much as I love the sea, the thought of raising our baby on land at a proper estate where we can give them whatever they desired sounds like heaven." Charlotte kissed his face all over as she spoke.

“Goddess, if a proper estate is what you want, then that is what you’ll have.” Hades kissed her forehead as he silently vowed to give Charlotte and their child whatever they asked for.

“Only as long as you’re still Hades in the bedroom.”

Hades threw back his head and laughed, placing both hands on the side of her head. “Whatever you wish, my pirate queen.”

Other Books by Joy Eileen

Rockstar Romance Slow Burn

Breaking Faith

Surviving Faith

Becoming Faith

Leap of Fate

Sports Romance Slow Burn

Balk

Paranormal Romance

Transparent

Ghost of Christmas Past

Matchmaking Ghost

Brother's Best Friend

Be Protective

Standalone MC age gap

Dirty Biker

MC

Zeus (age gap)

Marshal (fake marriage)

Banshee (rival gang's little sister)

Hawk (cop and mc)

Doc (president's little sister)

The making of The Pirate Queen

The making of this book was different than any other book I've ever written or even thought of. This book will go down as a legend in the Love and Devotion community. In June of 2025 at a Love and Devotion author signing in Burbank, Ca, I signed up for a reader engagement called Interactive Story Building. In a ballroom with about twelve tables each author picked a table and when the authors were settled the readers stampeded in. Thankfully, four amazing talented women sat at my table so I wouldn't be alone. Kc, Mj, Heather, Teri. We had no idea the adventure we were about to go on. The fantastic Meg went around to each table and had us pick one trait for her list, of course I picked funny. The only man in the room picked average sized feet, if you've ever seen a group of women collectively roll their eyes, you'll understand the beautiful sight we witnessed. Each table had an envelope with two pink cards and two green cards we had to choose from. I had the girls at the table pick a green and pink card and we had our troupe and our genre. Historical romance and childhood sweethearts. We also had to pick six of the traits on Megs list. Our table did not pick average sized feet. I asked the table if we should have a duke, an earl or something else and Teri asked, what about a pirate?

I need to confess when I was ten I would steal my grandma's harlequin bodice ripper novels reading them when I was way too young, and my favorite were the ones with pirates in them. It was the greatest suggestion and we went with it. We had one hour to write our story and together this book started to take shape. In the beginning the book did have a scene where there was no consent, I did change it to questionable consent as I wanted Charlotte to become the badass pirate queen she was meant to be. When our time was up, we had one minute to read our story. Our table ended up being the second to the last and unfortunately, I had to go after a Christian author and I was freaking out. When it was my turn, I told the story as fast as I could and before I got to the nonconsent part I screamed, I'm sorry Christian lady and then yelled pirate rape and the room went wild. It was a blast and after, I had many people ask me if I was going to turn our little idea into a book. This book wormed into my brain and although it isn't exactly how we fleshed it out in that room it still has the bones from that fateful day. Thank you Love and Devotion. Thank you, Kc, Mj, Heather, and Teri. And thank you to anyone who took the time to read this and enjoyed The Pirate Queen.

Made in the USA
Coppell, TX
13 May 2026

77138519R00194